PH[illegible]
BOHONIS

# Helen Whittaker

A 73 WINDSOR NOVEL

3rd Season Publications
www.3rdseason.ca

Designed by Crowe Creations
Cover design © 2015 Crowe Creations
Author photo © 2014 Sue Quinn

ISBN: 978-0-9920616-7-8

To my Thunder Bay card circle.
Miss you — even the long ride home.

"But, what happens when there's only one of us left?"
— Rose Nylund on The Golden Girls

73 Windsor: Helen Whittaker

# Chapter One

"I'm sorry, Mrs. Whittaker; I was rooting for you but, unfortunately, the final decision was not mine to make. I do wish you luck with your search."

"You just keep on rooting, Charlie Boy. That will really help." This said through gritted teeth after Helen shut the phone off.

Charles Kohanski had short-listed her after an initial interview for a bookkeeping position with Hanmer and Associates, a local engineering firm in Ottawa. In all fairness to Charlie, he was the first prospective employer to call her for a second interview. Mr. Hanmer and his associates had grilled her about her vision for her place within the firm in the next five and then ten years. To her credit, she had not told them her vision included retiring with a pension by that time. She knew her age of fifty-six was definitely not an attribute the partners considered an asset. After the interview, Helen realized they were looking for someone who in ten years would be trained and groomed for executive status. She was more than disappointed. Her name had been written all over this position or so she thought. However, she wouldn't panic, not yet anyway.

"Damn you, Edward Joseph Whittaker. How could you do this to me?" She dropped her head and was about to indulge in a soul-cleansing crying session when the phone rang once again.

She took several deep breaths before bringing the cordless receiver to her ear.

"Hi, Mom. How are you?" It was Ellie, her fountain of strength in all of this.

"I'm fine, sweetheart."

"How did the interview go yesterday?"

"The interview went fine. The outcome was lousy."

"Oh, Mom, you must be so disappointed. You had really positive vibes about this one."

"So much for vibes. So what does Andy think about his new braces?"

"Uh, oh. Changing the subject are we?"

"I guess I haven't had time to shake off the rejection. Maybe tomorrow I'll be ready to talk about it. Now what about my grandson's new mouth jewellery?"

"He almost refused to board the school bus this morning because of them."

"It seems to me his mother felt the same way about hers twenty-two years ago." Helen couldn't help the cynical laugh that followed.

Her daughter ignored it. "So what are your plans now? Any more prospects?"

Helen sighed. Ellie was not going to let up. "Not at the moment, but I'm sure something will come along. I can always pump gas at the Esso station down the road."

"Yeah, right. Aren't you the helpless little damsel who refuses to stop at self-serve stations because you can't even open your own gas cap?"

Silence.

"Okay, Mom, I get it. We're really hoping you'll reconsider what we talked about. We really need you here. I see it as a win, win situation for all of us."

"Darling, I appreciate your concern and your offer but I'm

not quite ready to become the resident grandmother. I still have things to do, horizons to explore. Besides, who will I play bridge with there? You and Willis hate cards."

"What I hate is to see you struggling when we really do want you here. You know Andy and Melanie would be so happy to have their grandma living here."

"We'll see, Ellie. I'll call you on the weekend." She patted the phone affectionately after breaking the connection.

Thank goodness her children had received excellent educations and were financially secure. The dream of a comfortable retirement was no longer a viable one for her however. If she was very careful she could probably stay in the condominium for four or five, possibly six months longer. Surely she would find employment before then. Her eyes were drawn to the wedding picture taken thirty-four years before. She wiped away a single tear that hung precariously from her lower lashes. She remembered the way Edward had laid out their lives with promises of three children. He had laughingly guaranteed her a girl and a boy and then one "it doesn't really matter" for the pot. The pot, however, had remained empty. After three miscarriages, they decided to count their blessings and be happy with the two healthy ones God had given them. Edward's laugh had been the first thing that caught her attention when they had met at a wedding reception. It had been his laugh that had won her heart and eventually broken it. His laugh and his promises. How had she been so blind?

*Well, Helen, you'll show him, won't you girl? You'll find a good paying job, get back on your feet and you will have the last laugh.* She was managing thus far to stay one step ahead of her monthly expenses, but if something didn't break soon her bank account would be dangerously low. As she was contemplating her next move, the doorbell rang.

When she opened the door, her neighbour, Olivia Kovacs,

was standing in the hallway. Olivia was the glamour girl of the building. At sixty-three, she looked younger than any of them and made no bones about discussing the high cost of body maintenance. Besides the tummy tucks, liposuction and facelifts, her well-cut hair was maintained in a warm honey-blond and weekly manicures and pedicures were deemed a necessity rather than a luxury. In her case the beauty didn't only go skin deep. Olivia was the best friend Helen had ever known. When Edward walked out and left her almost penniless, it was Olivia who had stayed and cried with her all night. The next day it was Olivia again who brought the darts to throw at the picture of Edward standing on his sailboat. It was also Olivia who was the first one there with a bottle of wine and two glasses when Edward was killed in an automobile accident two weeks later. That's when she learned that a small insurance policy and the condominium were all that was standing between her and bankruptcy. When the insurance money ran out she would have to sell the condo and live on the proceeds.

"Helen, I just came to tell you bridge will be delayed an hour today because Margaret's doctor was called away for an emergency surgery and he's running behind with his appointments."

"What's she seeing him for this time?"

"She thinks she may have Celiac disease." One corner of Olivia's mouth was twitching.

"Celiac disease? Good Lord, what brought this on?"

"You know she can't just suffer from heartburn or indigestion like everyone else. Her pain has to have designer status. There was a dietician on *The Marilyn Denis Show* the other day discussing menus and diets for persons suffering from the disease. Margaret was mesmerized and decided that's what she must have."

Helen stood open-mouthed staring at Olivia for a few seconds before the two women burst into laughter. "Oh my goodness, we shouldn't be poking fun at the poor woman. One of these days she might really be ill and we'll never forgive ourselves." Helen's remark didn't stop a second round of giggling however.

"I'll be at your place at two o'clock then instead of one. That will give me time to scan the newspaper and on-line ads and maybe get another application or two prepared."

"Helen, it breaks my heart to see you in this position. I just don't understand how … never mind, I know I shouldn't speak ill of the dead." Olivia rolled her eyes then hugged her friend and left.

Helen smiled. Olivia had told her many times how it bothered her that Helen was forced to look for work instead of continuing the lifestyle to which she had been accustomed. They had agreed that Edward, who Olivia always referred to as "that rotter of a husband", at least had done one thing right by leaving Helen's name as the beneficiary on his company insurance policy. Her friend was certain that had just been an oversight. Her remarks were not kind when it came to Edward Whittaker.

By ten minutes past two Helen, Olivia, Margaret McFarland and Sarah Eisenboch were well into the bidding process of their first hand of bridge. The only time their Thursday afternoon games were interrupted was during the month of February each year when Olivia and Sarah both headed south for a month of fun in the sun. Last winter Helen was to have traveled with them, however while still in the planning stage, she learned she had to cancel her plans—permanently.

"How was the interview, Helen?" It was Margaret who had told her the engineering firm was in need of a bookkeeper. Keeping her ears open in the doctor's waiting room three weeks earlier had paid off.

"The interview was just fine. Charlie and I hit it off big time."

"Charlie?"

"Charles Kohanski, their accountant and office manager."

"So you got the position then." Margaret was all smiles.

"No. No, I didn't, even though Charlie was really rooting for me. It seems that the big boys had visions slightly different from mine. Theirs entailed a younger, more malleable office worker who might eventually work into a clone of Charles and then take over his duties when he retires. Mine entailed getting enough years in to receive a company pension and be out of there before dementia sets in. Good Lord, I positively felt like Granny Smith sitting there being interviewed by three men almost young enough to be my sons."

The moans and pats on the arm didn't make her feel any better. In fact it made her resentful. Resentful as hell. Why was she forced to worry about keeping a roof over her head and not able to take vacations just because … just because the only man she had ever loved and trusted had duped her? He not only duped her, he had the audacity to die before she could kill him.

The afternoon passed with the usual jokes, tidbits of gossip and a few new women's novels critiqued.

"I hear a new man has moved into the Millers' condo. Supposed to be quite a hunk." Margaret was always looking for a man. She had been dependent on her husband while he was alive and more than once had commented that she did not like living alone.

"If he's a hunk Stella Jacobson will have already taken him some of her famous biscuits and clam chowder. Poor man, he won't know what hit him by the time she's finished plying him with food."

"Well that might work until he gets a look at Olivia. There's no way Stella can compete with her looks — or body." Helen winked at Olivia who drew back in disagreement.

"I'm not looking for anybody to tie me down. You know I

like my freedom and soon as you get a man buying you dinner or taking you to a play, next thing you know he's asking where you're going every time you step out of the building. No thank-you."

"What about you, Helen? If you had a man again, you wouldn't have to worry about looking for work."

"I'll take my chances on working. If I end up selling coffee and donuts over a counter it would be preferable to placing all my eggs in some man's basket again. I'm about as receptive to another man in my life as Olivia is. We'll leave the field open to you two. And Stella." She smiled at Margaret and Sarah.

"Oh, my goodness, look at the time. I've got to get to the drugstore and pick up my prescription." Margaret pulled her compact from her purse and reapplied some lipstick.

"I'll ride down with you if you like. I didn't pick up my mail today. I better check my e-mails when I come back too. Who knows, maybe I'll have another job interview somewhere tomorrow."

"Helen, don't brush off too lightly the idea of a man to support you. There are some good ones out there." Margaret patted Helen's arm.

"I don't care how many good men are out there. I'm not interested in snagging one, dating one, or even talking to one. I will support myself no matter what it takes."

❣❣❣

Margaret left Helen in the lobby of their building while she went next door to the pharmacy. As she was about to pull the heavy door to let herself back in, a man with the darkest brown eyes pulled it open and held it while she stepped through. She smiled and was about to thank him when the magnificent eyes moved beyond her and changed from startled disbelief to something much warmer. The corners of his wide, soft mouth lifted into a gorgeous smile.

"Helen? Helen, is that really you?" His voice was soft and questioning.

As Margaret turned to see if it was their Helen he was addressing, he brushed by her leaving a mild citrus fragrance in his wake. Helen looked up from her mail to see who was calling her. She didn't seem to recognize him.

"It's me. Gerald. Gerald Mercier. I know it's been a long time but surely you haven't forgotten me."

"Gerald." Helen's voice was a mere whisper. "Oh my gosh, Gerald." A louder whisper this time with a hint of a quiver. Then before Margaret knew what was happening, Helen had dropped her mail and was in his arms, crying.

# Chapter Two

"You mean she was actually crying?"

"And hanging on to him for dear life."

"It was the new man? The one who bought the Millers' condo?"

"The hunk himself."

Nobody had seen Helen since the scene in the foyer. It was now ten o'clock, almost bedtime and she wasn't answering her phone or her doorbell.

"We can't just knock on his door and ask if she's there."

"The way she was hugging him, she must have known him well even though she didn't seem to recognize him at first."

"Okay. We'll let it go for now but I'll be calling her first thing in the morning. You can bet on it."

The two women bid each other a hesitant goodnight. By an unspoken mutual agreement the four friends kept tabs on each other on a daily basis. It was not done out of idle curiosity but because one of their neighbours had been mugged and beaten in a nearby park the year before. No one had missed the poor soul until she was found unconscious and badly injured almost forty-eight hours later. She had survived but only after a long recovery process. So it had just evolved that they called each other in rotation morning and evening.

"Helen should have called and let one of us know she would be late getting home. I hope she hasn't suffered a stroke, or worse." Margaret, the hypochondriac, always thought the worst.

"I'm sure she's fine." Olivia whispered as she closed the door to her own apartment.

❣❣❣

"I was told there was a hunk now living in this condo. Little did I know it was a hunk from my past." Helen took the cup of tea Gerald had prepared.

"A hunk? Get out. Women still use that term?" His deep, sexy laugh exposed a dimple in his left cheek. "I thought men my age could expect at best to be called distinguished or said to have 'aged well'. In my case, I've never been the former and I'm not sure about the latter."

"What brings you to Ottawa, Gerald? Or have you been living here all these years?"

"I just recently moved here from Montreal. I retired and wanted to live closer to my son."

"Retired from what?"

"From plying the international waters."

"Ah, yes, you left Sault Ste. Marie to work on the lake freighters. I didn't know you had made a career out of it."

"I did. What about you, Helen? How long have you lived here?"

"I came here as a bride. My husband was from Ottawa and worked for the federal government. We had been engaged for a few months and when the opportunity for a promotion and transfer here became available, we decided to marry immediately and move together."

❣❣❣

His eyes took in her medium brown hair that still had the same soft curl as it had as a teenager. Her skin was flawless except for the beauty mark just below and to the right of her long straight nose. The smoky-taupe eye shadow she wore made her brown eyes so dark, he couldn't distinguish her pupils. Her lashes were just as thick and dark as he remembered and her soft full mouth had a hint of lipstick residue around the edge. When she cleared her throat and their eyes connected once again, he saw amusement and something else reflected in hers.

"Sorry, I guess I was staring. I can't believe that after all these years you've hardly changed, hardly aged. My God, Helen, how long has it been, twenty-five years?"

"At least. It was your brother's funeral."

"Yes, I remember. You came to the service but couldn't stay. We didn't even have the opportunity to talk other than you shaking my hand and offering condolences." He remembered how her slender hand had felt in his and how he had wished it could have lingered there. He had always wanted more from her than he received, more than he knew he deserved.

"Well, I can't believe you recognized me after all this time. Now that I'm standing here talking to you, I can see the old you but I would have walked right by you in the lobby."

"I had a slight advantage. My sister sent me a newspaper picture of you taken about fifteen years ago when you were in Sault Ste. Marie for a convention of some kind. You were the big cheese as I recall."

"Oh my goodness. I'm surprised Doreen would have recognized me. I didn't think she even knew my married name. Yes, I chaired a national committee for a women's organization and attended a fundraiser there."

"Helen, are you still married?" He asked hesitantly even though she wore no wedding ring.

"No. Edward died in a car accident last fall."

"I'm sorry. I'm sure you must still find it difficult without it."

"Actually we had separated prior to that. I should say he had separated."

"He left you?"

"Yes. It came out of the blue. I think you could say he 'blind-sided me'."

"I'm sorry Helen, but I have to say it. He must have been a fool."

"Well, let's just say he had developed a penchant for much younger women. Make that singular — one younger woman."

He took her hand and brought it to his lips. "I repeat. The man was a fool." He noticed her shoulders slump and her eyes lower. There was more to this than she was telling but he didn't want to push her. He had no right to ask too many personal questions. He could see that she was hurting and selfishly hoped she wasn't still in love with the man even though he was gone.

"Can I buy you dinner? We have a lot of catching up to do. I'm afraid if I let you go now, you might slip away."

She laughed and he loved the sound of it. "I won't be slipping away, Gerald. I live upstairs and hope not to have to move — for a while, anyway."

He let that last phrase go for the time being. "Good. I see you have your purse with you. Why don't we just go around the corner and enjoy some chicken and pasta in the bistro?"

"That sounds wonderful." He noticed her eyes slide over his body. He was careful to stay in good shape and hoped she wasn't disappointed in what she saw. She connected once again with his dark brown eyes that he knew were almost a match to her own. "Gerald, I can't believe you are here."

He grinned as he followed her through the door. It would appear she was genuinely happy to see him. He had never thought he would see this day, had given up hope years ago of ever taking Helen to dinner.

Out on the street she slid her arm through his as they walked to the corner. Almost as tall as him in her high heels, they made a striking couple as they entered the restaurant. Gerald asked for a quiet booth where they could continue to catch up on all the years they had been separated. He told her he had not married until he was into his thirties, was father to one son who recently graduated from university and was practicing dentistry here in Ottawa. His wife had developed diabetes and had died from kidney failure nine years ago just before their son had graduated from high school.

He knew she had taken an office position with one the major steel plants in Sault Ste. Marie. His mother and sister had always kept him abreast of the lives of all his hometown friends. They had also told him of Helen's marriage and her move away from home. Helen filled in the gaps, telling him she had a daughter living in Kingston and a son who had recently moved to Vancouver. She also had three grandchildren she didn't get to see often enough. Her parents were both dead, her father having died shortly after her move away and her mother just a couple of years ago. She didn't go into the details of her marriage or separation to and from Edward.

Before they knew it, a couple of hours had slipped by and it was time to leave. "Gerald, it seems like the years have been stripped away. You are just as easy to talk with now as when we were in school. I haven't enjoyed a meal or someone's company this much in a very long time. Thank you for inviting me." She squeezed his hand as they slid out of the booth.

"I hope we can renew our friendship, Helen. I don't know whether I was more startled or happy to see you standing by the mailboxes this afternoon. I could hardly believe my eyes."

They walked slowly back to their building, each wishing the distance were a little longer. "I don't know about you, but I'm ready to take a stroll around the block and try to work off some of that pasta, Helen. Care to join me?"

"Yes. It's such a warm evening, it would be a shame to go inside this early. We could even walk a little way through the market."

"I haven't had an opportunity to see much of our capital city yet, will you give me a guided tour one of these days?"

"I would love to. Living here all these years, I tend to take the beauty of the city for granted. I'm overdue for a refresher tour."

There were a number of buskers working the market and the unusually warm, late-spring evening had drawn many city dwellers out to enjoy the sights and sounds. The next couple of hours seemed to pass as quickly as had their time in the bistro. Reluctantly, they returned to their building and entered the spacious foyer.

"What's your condo number, Helen?"

"I'm on the ninth floor — 906. I'll write my phone number down for you as well." She took a small note pad from her purse and scribbled it out for him.

He waited till the elevator door opened at her floor and gave her cheek a brush with his lips. She startled him however, by taking his face in both her hands and planting a soft, warm kiss on his lips. "We've known each other far too long, Gerald Mercier, for just a peck on the cheek."

Brown eyes locked on brown eyes. "If she only knew …" he thought as the elevator doors closed.

# Chapter Three

"You couldn't even take a minute to let one of us know that you were going out with an old boyfriend?" It was obvious Margaret was having difficulty pretending to be chagrined when her eyes were alight with curiosity. "Olivia and I were upset, worried that you might have fallen, or worse."

Helen found it difficult to keep the amusement from her own eyes. "I ran into him downstairs, you know that, and after some tea in his apartment, we decided to go out for dinner. It was completely spur of the moment."

"It would have taken less than a minute to call and tell one of us."

"Less than a minute? I don't think so. By the time you would have gone through giving me the third degree, I would have missed dinner and had to settle for a night-cap with him."

Indignation showed on Margaret's face but before she could think of a suitable retort, her features softened and her lips curved into a smile. "You're probably right. I was astonished to see you in the arms of the hunk, maybe even a little bit jealous. Are you going to tell me about it … him … your evening? I'll beat it out of you if you don't."

Helen grinned at her friend. "He was my first love. Gave me my first kiss and I can still feel it." She brought her fingertips to her lips. "He was the kindest, most gentle male I've ever known. Just a boy actually."

"What happened?"

"I don't really know. He drifted away from me. We had always been close but as we got into our junior and senior years in high school I used to catch him staring at me sometimes in classes. When I questioned him what he was thinking about he would just pass it off as daydreaming. He left home as soon as he graduated from high school and went to work on the lake freighters. I only ever saw him once after that, just a brief encounter on a street downtown. Then I married, moved away and happened to be visiting back home when I saw his brother's obituary in the newspaper. I barely had time to make it to the service before my plane was due to take off. I shook his hand, gave him my condolences and left. That's all there is to tell. I never saw him again until yesterday."

"So now what?"

"What do you mean?"

"The way his eyes glowed when he spotted you, I think he was happy to see you. Extremely happy."

"We are old friends who haven't seen each other in years. Of course we were happy to see each other … and to answer your question, we will continue to be friends and because we live in the same building, we'll probably see each other regularly."

"Boy, is Stella gonna be pissed."

"Margaret, watch your language. That's not a term a lady uses." Then she winked and couldn't help smiling as she walked her friend to the door.

No more job interviews were forthcoming so after a couple of days, Helen sat at the desk in her den with a calculator, several files, and her most recent bank statement. After several hours of research on the world-wide-web and two phone calls to her banker, she placed her pen on the desk and buried her head in her hands. After cutting her budget to the absolute minimum, which meant cancelling her newspaper subscription, changing her cable to the basic package, reducing her housekeeper's visits to once a month for a thorough cleaning instead of bi-weekly, she then changed some of her remaining investments into more stable saving certificates and bonds. Her calculator was smoking by the time she concluded that she could remain solvent for seven more months. That was barring any unforeseen expenses such as appliance, car or health breakdowns. She was still four years away from eligibility to collect even the most basic government pension and nine years away from receiving old age security.

"Well, old girl, you've got approximately a three year gap in there." She had thought one avenue might be to re-mortgage her condo. The only problem with that she was reminded by her banker, is that you are required to have an income from which to make the payments. "Dumb rule, must have been made by a man." She had felt foolish upon being told this. As a bookkeeper she had this information stored in a deep recess of her brain but in her desperation had overlooked it.

She turned to the calculator once more to estimate what earnings would be required to help her money stretch for three years. In the end, she realized it could be done, even at just slightly more than minimum wage, if she worked *almost* full time. Maybe it was possible to lower her sights from an office position to one in retail. Of course that would mean being on her feet all day instead of sitting at a desk. "It might do me some good," she thought. "It would definitely do my butt some good."

She went through the newspaper once again, this time looking at retail positions instead of office. There certainly were more to choose from. After circling several in the paper and checking out several listings on-line, she set about revising her resume to look attractive to employers in the retail field. With determination in her step, she descended to the mailbox in the foyer later that evening with several envelopes in her hand. The sound of them dropping to the bottom appeared to have a more positive sound. Maybe, just maybe, between those and the electronic CV's she had sent, something might open up. She patted the top of the box and turned to see Gerald approaching the door of the building.

Her heart warmed at the sight of his deeply coloured complexion. He always did have slightly olive-toned skin even as a youngster, probably from his French parents. The many years at sea seemed to have given him a permanent tan. She was surprised his face didn't have the worn and weathered look that other men in his profession had. It must be in the genes she thought as she watched him move toward her. He still hadn't noticed her, which gave her the opportunity to give him the once over without being watched in return. He didn't quite reach six feet she thought, but he appeared taller because of his stature. She remembered he had always been about ten pounds heavier than he should be but he had the frame to carry it. He had matured well.

"Oh, Helen, I was just thinking about you." With his head down slightly to watch his footing on the freshly cleaned and wet slate floor, he almost bumped right into her.

"Really? You did look deep in thought. Were you thinking that it might be nice if I were to invite you to dinner tomorrow night?"

"Something along that vein. Actually, I was hoping we might go to see the tulips at Parliament Hill and grab a bite to eat in the market before a walk along the canal. I understand it's supposed to be a warm, sunny day tomorrow."

"Your idea does sound more pleasant and I haven't seen the tulips yet. Will you let me give you a rain check for the dinner?"

"I would love to have you cook dinner for me, Helen. In fact that has pretty well

been a fantasy of mine."

"Really?"

"You bet, ever since we were six years old and I used to

watch you and Betty Ann Campbell have tea parties in her front yard."

"You remember that? I had almost forgotten about dressing up and pretending we were rich ladies married to kings. You should have joined us. We usually had chocolate chip cookies that Betty Ann's mother baked."

"If I had only known. I always thought those were mud pies." He smiled as he moved closer to her. "It wasn't usually cookies I was thinking about though. My thoughts were usually on how to get you alone so I could kiss that sunburned nose of yours."

"At six years old? My dad would have tanned your hide."

"That's what kept me from doing it." The smile left his face.

The elevator opened and Stella Jacobson stepped out. Without even looking at Helen, she immediately laid her hand on Gerald's arm and gave him a smile that would out dazzle the sun. "Did you enjoy the apple pie, Gerald?"

"Yes, I did, thoroughly. Thank you. I've been meaning to return your dish." He glanced at Helen uncomfortably, as she stepped into the elevator and wiggled her fingers in a parting gesture.

❣❣❣

"Didn't I tell you? I knew she wouldn't pass up an opportunity to get her fingernails firmly planted in a good-looking man before anyone else could." Sarah was gloating over her accurate forecast.

"You're forgetting one thing though. He's not interested in her. He has his cap set for our Helen, so that man-hungry pants-chaser needn't even bother."

"Whoa. I told you that he's an old friend. That doesn't mean we are, or intend to be, romantically inclined. Besides I don't make very good apple pies." The amusement Helen felt at Sarah's prediction being true shone in her eyes and her smile. "I'm not about to become involved in a bake-off to see who can win the heart or stomach of Gerald Mercier."

"You won't have to, Helen. I'll bet he invites you to spend an evening with him again before the week is over." Olivia folded her arms in front of her as the others nodded their agreement.

"Oh, my. I guess I shouldn't tell you then that we're spending tomorrow afternoon and evening together. You'll have us married in no time. Poor Gerald, that unsuspecting man just doesn't stand a chance ... and what about Stella? Will she survive the disappointment? All that flour wasted, not to mention the high price of apples."

"She'll get over it. Now tell us, when do we get to meet this hunk? Margaret is the only one who has actually seen him and she gives him a ten and a half. How about it, are we going to have to follow you and accidentally ambush you tomorrow afternoon? Is he really better than a ten?"

Before Helen could answer, her doorbell rang. A sheepish looking Gerald stood in the hallway when she opened the door.

"I'm sorry, Helen. I don't know why that woman insists on bringing me food. First it was soup and biscuits and then ..." His sheepish expression turned to one of embarrassment when he saw three attractive women staring at him like he was dinner and they were starving.

Taking stock of the situation, she took his arm and walked him inside as she explained that her friends were just leaving. She introduced each one by name and allowed them time to shake hands before she ushered each lady out the door. As she attempted to close it behind them, each one gave her a thumbs-up and Olivia even managed a wink before being shut out.

"Why do I get the feeling I arrived right in the middle of something?"

"Actually you arrived in the middle of their departure. They had overstayed their welcome."

He gave her a lingering stare but didn't question her further. "We didn't settle a time to tour the tulips." His eyes were taking in the tasteful decorating and soft ambience of Helen's foyer and living room. It felt peaceful and warm — a place a man could relax in and yet there was a feminine delicacy to it as well. The furniture was sturdy and man-sized, but the colours were subtle and softened the masculinity. A delicate fragrance, her fragrance, was barely noticeable. He realized Helen had spoken and was embarrassed when he had to ask her to repeat herself.

"I wondered if you wanted to change the plans to a late lunch downtown, and then we can take our time sightseeing. I can have dinner prepared ahead of time to enjoy later when we return."

"That sounds absolutely perfect. I'll bring some wine to chill while we're out."

"How many hotdogs can you eat, two or three?"

"Pardon?"

"Just so I know how many wieners to thaw out."

He smiled. "You haven't changed one single bit. You used to drive my sister crazy with your warped sense of humour. I'll come for you around two tomorrow afternoon then."

❣❣❣

When he closed the door behind him, Helen felt a strange sense of foreboding. Was she getting more involved than she intended? Did he have only renewing their friendship in mind? She was determined to remain independent. "Once burned, twice shy," she repeated to herself. I will never again allow myself to be deceived by a man. She knew she should not allow herself to become cynical, but hindsight would have come in handy when she had allowed Edward to talk her into giving up her career and volunteering her time instead of getting paid for it. None of his colleagues' wives worked she was told. It made him look less successful because she had a nine-to-five job while the other women enjoyed playing cards, meeting for long lunches, and volunteering at the hospital. She had allowed herself to be swayed and before long, she too was playing cards, enjoying lunches with her friends and volunteering at the children's hospital. She had become comfortable in her role as wife of a successful investment planner with an international firm after he left his position with the government. She had turned a blind eye to his increasing late nights and his business trips to Toronto. When the bills had stopped coming to the house, he had assured her that his own bookkeeper was paying them through the business and separating the business portion from personal for income tax purposes. Ya, right. What a fool she had been. She hadn't even become suspicious when he started making excuses for staying overnight at the office. Well okay, maybe she had wondered a little, but her Edward was so attentive and loving, always had been, when they were together. He would never hurt her, never risk their marriage on even a flirtation let alone a fling — until Irene Urquhart came upon the scene. Irene with the baby blue eyes, the flaming red hair and the body that was every woman's envy.

After Edward and Irene had torn her life apart, she had sworn she would never trust another man. Now Gerald was rattling the key to her heart after all these years. Sweet, gentle Gerald. He would never hurt her. *Who are you kidding? He walked out of your life once, didn't he?*

She wiped a tear from her eye as she remembered.

*Okay. Enjoy his company, remember old times, but if he starts coming on strong, lose him.* With the resolve to dump him at the first sign of anything romantic, she answered the telephone when it began to ring.

"Hello, Helen. This is Irene Urquhart. We have to talk."

# Chapter Four

"You have a lot of nerve calling me. If you want to talk phone my lawyer." She couldn't believe the nerve of the bitch.

"I can do that of course but I thought I'd save you the hefty fee if I could."

"Call her. I'll pay it." She slammed the phone down.

It took a number of long, deep breaths before she was calm enough to even wonder what the calculating redhead wanted from her now. *She's knows I have no money and surely she doesn't want my first-born.* After a moment's thought and remembering that her first-born is a thirty-two year old clone of his dad … *No, don't even go there, Helen. Nicholas hates her more than any of us.*

Their son had let Edward know exactly what his feelings were about his affair with Irene. They had almost come to blows and Nicholas had not spoken to his father again. When Edward was killed in the car accident, any slight remorse he might have felt about the estrangement between he and his father soon reversed itself when the truth became evident about the financial situation in which Helen had been left. He had sought out Irene at his father's office and calmly made a brief statement. "You were not content only to steal my son's grandfather, you stole his inheritance as well. Not only the money, but the legacy of honesty he should have been left. May you and my father both rot in hell."

When Nicholas had learned his dad had been entrenched in a hotel room with Irene and had lied, not once but twice, about his reasons for missing Benjamin's sixth birthday and then his first school Christmas concert, it had been all Helen could do to keep her son from physically attacking his father. When he calmed down he had cried in his mother's arms.

"How could he do that, Mom? How could he disappoint his own little grandson by lying about being at a client's while he's screwing some bitch half his age, for god's sake? This can't be the same dad that used to drive me to my ball games and help me with my math homework."

It had broken her heart to see him so upset with his father. He had barely recovered from that hurt when Edward had died and Nicholas learned that his father had squandered his parents' life savings on this same young redhead. That's when he had paid a visit to his father's girlfriend.

Now Irene was saying they had to talk. She couldn't help but wonder what the woman wanted but she had no desire to have a conversation with her. Life was distressing enough at the moment without adding her husband's mistress to the mix. Determined to let their lawyers deal with it, she settled on the sofa to watch a rerun of *Law and Order*.

The next morning she prepared a recipe for breaded spare-ribs and pre-cooked it for heating in the oven upon their return. Her Caesar salad always won wave reviews so she tore the lettuce and prepared the dressing. It would only take a few minutes for a couple of potatoes to bake in the microwave. For dessert she had ice cream and decided on some wonderful French pastries that were available from a vendor in the market. That done, she had enough time to have a leisurely bath and pedicure before Gerald would arrive for their afternoon and evening out.

She was surprised none of her friends had dropped by with questions about her "date for a day". Perhaps they were upset with her for ushering them out so quickly the day before. Olivia hadn't said anything when she checked up on her this morning though, nor had Sarah when Helen had followed through with her call. They already knew not to call tonight and interrupt her late dinner. She assumed they'd be around in the morning full of questions.

When she opened the door to Gerald at precisely two, she felt a familiar warmth at his easy smile and dark eyes. The fact that he never seemed aware of his own good looks only added to the male charm he naturally exuded. His smile had always comforted her, even as children. Somehow, the world had always seemed right when he was around — safe and full. The grey golf-style, short-sleeved shirt and black trousers matched the grey and black mix of his hair. He carried a grey jacket and in his free hand was a bottle of red wine.

"I wasn't sure what was on the menu but I always enjoy a good red and hoped you might too." He brushed her with a kiss as he closed the door behind him.

"Red is fine. I'll put it in the kitchen and we can be on our way. Did you wear good walking shoes?"

After a short discussion they decided to take Gerald's car and include a drive past the homes of the Prime Minister and Governor General in their outing. After lunch at a restaurant on Sparks Street they left the car parked in a public lot and walked to the Parliament buildings. Helen was sorry she hadn't brought a camera to have someone take a picture of her with her old friend. "We'll bring a camera next time, Helen. I hope this won't be the last time we're together on the streets of Ottawa."

"No, I suppose it won't be." She looked at him inquisitively. "You're here for the long haul then?"

"Yes, I am. I bought the condominium with the thought in mind of seeing a little more of my son, but he's so engaged in setting up his new practice that he hardly has time for me. He was very relieved to learn I had met an old friend to hang out with. I think it eased his conscience somewhat. Although the last thing I want is for him to think he has to babysit his old man."

"You're lucky to have him close. My son lives so far away right now and I miss him terribly. He and his family have only been gone six months but it seems much longer."

"What took him out to the west coast?"

"Computers. He has an engineering degree in computer sciences. He had been working for one of the major resellers of computers here in Ottawa but received an offer from a firm in Vancouver that seemed almost too good to be true. After checking it out and comparing the cost of living and in spite of the higher accommodation costs he decided it was a good deal and accepted it. He has one son who is in the first grade, whose life wasn't upset too badly by the move. His wife, Rebecca, is a nurse and decided she could do that just as easily out there as here. Consequently, they were gone within a month. They had been renting a townhouse in the west end so it was easy for them to pick up and go."

His eyes told her he was feeling her pain, but he managed to smile. "So no one will worry if I don't bring you back until midnight then."

She laughed. "I also have a daughter who lives in Kingston but she's usually in bed well before midnight. But … I have three friends who were already worried senseless when I didn't answer my phone or doorbell hours after being seen in the arms of a strange man in our lobby."

"Oh, oh. Please tell me you don't belong to a Ya Ya Sisterhood?"

"I've already told them not to even think about calling tonight."

"Hmm, Helen, what *do* you have in mind?" He wiggled his eyebrows and nuzzled her ear.

"Whatever it is … or isn't, is none of their business."

"I see." The amusement shone in his eyes. "Well, I've never been one to kiss and tell. I think even you remember that. So whatever does or doesn't happen tonight, will never go beyond my sealed lips. I promise."

"You kept your mouth shut only because you were afraid of my father, not because of some ingrained chivalry, Gerald Mercier. However, it might get them off my back if they thought we were involved."

"Why are they on your back?"

She hesitated, almost telling him of her financial situation. Pride kept her from disclosing anything more however. "They think I should have a man in my life."

"Do they? Have men in their lives, that is?"

"No. Margaret and Sarah would like one, but Olivia is too independent. They all however are delighted that I'm 'seeing someone'."

"And what about you, Helen, would you like a man in your life?"

"Absolutely not!" The stunned look on his face immediately had her back-tracking. "What I mean is that I'm independent too. I was married for a long time and I'm enjoying being on my own. My daughter has been begging me to move closer to her so I can be a part of their lives, she says, but I know she wants them to be more a part of mine."

"That's a bad thing because …?"

"I just told you. I'm enjoying my independence."

"So by pretending to have an affair with me you believe your friends would quit trying to match you up with someone."

She slid her arm through his as they continued their walk. "I don't want to pretend anything, Gerald. I am extremely happy that an old friend has come back into my life and I want to enjoy that friendship without any outside interference. Am I being selfish or asking too much?"

He put his hand over hers on his arm and gently squeezed it. "Not at all. If we have a friendly affair we won't even tell them." He wiggled his eyebrows again.

❦❦❦

"Helen, I can't remember enjoying ribs more. Your mother's cooking lessons paid off just as she said they would. I remember you and Elsie Dudnick getting upset when your mothers made you come in and help with the meals while Betty Ann was allowed to stay outside."

"Yeh, well, I was always jealous of the way Betty Ann's mother spoiled her. I hope she married some rich guy who could afford live-in housekeepers, nannies and cooks." She took their plates to the kitchen and returned with coffee. "This is not one of my mother's recipes, however she did teach me the basics. I love cooking and have attended several specialty cooking classes over the years."

Her shoulders slumped and her eyes closed for a few seconds. "Cooking for one is boring. I usually invite my friends in the building over for dinner once a month and try out new recipes on them. Gerald, I'll be happy to try some new dishes out on you too, if you don't mind playing guinea pig once in a while."

"I'll look forward to it. In fact, you give me a list and I'll be happy to go to the market for the ingredients."

When Helen finished tidying the kitchen she joined him on the sofa. "For someone who never came back home, you sure do have a lot of memories." Turning to face him, she asked, "Why didn't you come back, Gerald? Your family was all there."

"I guess there were too many memories, not all of them good. I couldn't come back. I … just couldn't." He stood and walked to the window. When he didn't move for several long minutes, Helen walked to him and lightly stroked the back of his shirt.

"I can't imagine what kind of memories would keep you away. You always seemed to love everything and everybody, Gerald. You were the only one I could always count on being there for me. I missed you terribly when you left. When I asked your mother where I could write to you, she told me you moved around too much and that even she had to wait for your postcards or your few phone calls." She remembered the pain back then when the thought of never seeing him again was almost too much to bear.

"I'll tell you about it someday, Helen, but for tonight I just want to enjoy your company and possibly one of those pastries I watched you buy." He looked wistfully toward the kitchen.

"Men and their stomachs. Maybe I should take some lessons from Stella. I'll get more coffee and the pastries."

He watched her lithe body as she walked bare-legged and bare-footed back to the kitchen. She probably didn't weigh much more than she had as a teenager. She'd always been taller than her friends and active in school sports. Track and field had been her strength and running had kept her lean. It was the second hardest thing he had done in his life, to walk away and not say good-bye to her. The hardest had been not returning. Growing up, she was always there and he had taken for granted she would always be there, be a part of his life. When the reality of life was forced upon him, he knew that wasn't going to be the case. It had taken him almost fifteen years to find someone else with whom he was comfortable sharing his life. It was unfortunate that their time together had been cut short. Now, here he was, once again with Helen. Beautiful Helen. His fear had always been that she had hated him for running away, if not immediately, then grown to do so over the years. He should have had a greater understanding of her than that. She was not a hateful person.

❣❣❣

"There are three different kinds, so I cut them in half and you can sample all three if you like. I think I noticed you drinking your coffee black but I can get the cream and sugar if you like." She set the tray on the round coffee table in front of him.

"Black is fine and the pastry looks so good I may just try all three. Are you not joining me?"

"I'll have some coffee but I'm trying to keep desserts out of my diet."

"Why? You certainly don't have a weight problem."

"I'm trying to compete with twenty-year-olds in the job market so I don't dare allow myself any rolls around the middle."

"Why are you in the job market?"

Too late she realized she had opened a can of worms. She took a deep breath. "I'm looking for a job, preferably part-time but I'll take whatever is available and I'm finding the competition pretty stiff."

"If you have too much time on your hands, Helen, I'm more than willing to keep you busy."

"Thanks, Gerald, but it's more than that. I spoke without thinking by bringing the subject up. Since Edward died I need to increase my income a little if I'm to keep my condominium. I'm not *that* old that I can't work a few hours a week but the market is definitely geared to the younger woman."

"Helen, I don't want to pry but looking around your home and admiring your wardrobe I wouldn't have guessed you weren't financially secure."

"I was one of those foolish wives, secure in her marriage, who allowed her husband to look after all the finances. When Edward died, I learned that he and his girlfriend had broken our bank account as well as our marriage. I was left with the condominium, a small company life insurance policy and debt, lots and lots of debt."

He wrapped an arm around her and lifted her chin so he could see into her eyes. "Helen, I am really and truly sorry. You don't deserve this. I said before that the man was a fool, but now I change that to a greedy, heartless fool." He leaned away from her. "Is this why you don't want a man in your life again?"

"That's a big part of it. I can't believe I was so stupid not to see the signs, not to ask more questions, not to … to …" She couldn't help herself. The tears came.

He pulled her to him and kissed the top of her head. "Oh, brown-eyes. I wish I could have the satisfaction of punching him out for hurting you. I feel so inadequate sitting here, not able to do anything."

"Nobody's called me brown-eyes since you went away." She sniffed and smiled through her tears. "You *are* doing something, Gerald. You're listening and offering moral support."

"Your friends can offer you that. I want to do more."

"My friends' arms aren't as strong as yours and not one of them even offered to kiss the top of my head." She moved back and looked straight at him. "I didn't intend for you to know my situation. It's embarrassing for me and I certainly didn't want you feeling sorry for me."

"What I'm feeling for you certainly isn't pity, Helen. What kind of job are you looking for?"

"I thought it would be easy for me to go back to office work but somewhere along the way they changed the rules. They even changed the way they conduct interviews. Now you have to have a plan, a vision of where you and the company are going to be in a year, five years, even ten years. There is no such thing as just the promise of showing up on time five days a week and putting in an honest day's work anymore. You have to contribute and be ready to grow with the company. You have to chart *your* place in *their* future. Hell, I thought the fact that I was beyond childbearing years would be a big plus for me. Was I wrong! Having attended the same school and/or using the same day-care as the boss or his or her spouse is quintessential to landing any position. In other words, I'm outdated."

"So what else can you do?"

"I did give that some thought and decided I can do retail. I have good fashion instincts to sell women's clothing and I keep up to date on the latest books. I think I can sell jewellery or china and crystal just as well or better than the young competition out there. I've certainly had more years to enjoy the product and actually use it."

"Do you have any interviews arranged?"

"No, but I only put my resumes in the mail and on-line yesterday. I don't anticipate hearing from any employers for a few more days."

"Wonderful, then tomorrow shall we visit the Museum of Man and the National Art Gallery? We should visit what we can before you start on a new career."

The tears were gathering behind her eyelids once more. "Thank you for not laughing at me."

"Laughing? What is there to laugh at?"

"At someone my age having to start all over in that jungle out there."

"Helen, I have nothing but admiration for you. Instead of feeling sorry for yourself and your situation, you're going out there and doing something about it. I remember someone once was quoted as saying 'If you can't change your fate — change your attitude'. That takes guts and I want to do whatever I can to help you. I'll even pack your lunch bag for you if you let me."

Now the tears did come. "Gerald, hold me. I want to feel your arms around me just like old times."

He lifted her chin and gazed at her lips before lowering his mouth to them. "You have no idea how many times I've wished I could do that. I'm the one that can't believe I'm here with you."

She touched his dimple, his chin, then ran her finger around his ear. "You were always my protector. Always there to pick me up when I fell down. You have no idea how many times I thought about you over the years. I even wondered sometimes whether you were still alive. You just seemed to disappear from the face of the earth. When I saw you the other day, I couldn't believe my eyes."

The tears eased as Gerald held her and rested his lips on her forehead. His eyes strayed to the picture of a young Helen dressed in a white wedding gown and the smiling Edward standing beside her. *You asshole. You didn't deserve her.* He couldn't help his thoughts as he silently cursed the man and vowed to make it all up to her. He wanted to wrap her in his arms and keep her secure forever. He also remembered that she had always been an extremely proud person."

# Chapter Five

Three days later, Helen was happy to report to Gerald and her friends she would be starting work the next afternoon at Spencer's Fine Jewellery in the Rideau Centre. It was only fifteen hours a week for now, but she had her foot in the door at least. Her hopes were high that those hours would be extended as summer loomed closer and the tourism season blossomed.

She was to work two afternoons per week from two until six and Saturdays from ten until six with an hour break for lunch. Gerald had offered to drive her to work so that she wouldn't have to worry about parking. When he dropped her at the entrance to the mall, he handed her a brown lunch bag with a muffin in it. "For your coffee break." He winked and brushed her cheek with his lips. "Go get 'em, brown-eyes."

"I'm quite nervous. The only retail sales I've done are at the tuck shop in the Children's Hospital and there isn't even a cash register there."

"You're familiar with computers, Helen, it will be a piece of cake. You don't look nervous. In fact, you exude confidence the way you're dressed." He gave her hand a squeeze before she eased herself out the door.

❣❣❣

Watching her walk into the entrance, he couldn't help but be proud of this beautiful woman who was starting another phase of her life at the age of fifty-six. It was a pride mixed with discontent. He had found her at a time when she couldn't enjoy life. Her pride placed her in the position of spending her days fending for herself instead of enjoying her days with him and her friends. *Patience, my man. Moral support is what she wants right now, not financial. Give her time.*

❣❣❣

Her day went without incident, in fact her sales were comparable to her workmate's. Jennifer Healey was a petite woman in her mid-forties, who had worked in the store for eight years. Helen learned that her predecessor left when her husband was transferred to his company's head office in Calgary. She also learned that they didn't usually take coffee breaks as such. There was a coffee maker and a couple of chairs in the back room where the staff could relax as long as one of them remained on the floor. When six o'clock rolled around she was ready to take her shoes off and rest her aching feet. She knew she would have to wear a flatter heel on Saturday or she wouldn't survive the longer day. Gerald waiting at the entrance was a welcome sight.

As soon as she opened the car door, she could smell Chinese food. "I didn't think you would feel like cooking when you got home. Do you mind if I join you?"

"Of course I don't. I love Chinese by the way."

She removed her shoes and pantyhose and changed into a pair of Capri pants and a loose-fitting cotton knit sweater. By the time she joined Gerald again, he had warmed the various foods in the microwave and had the table set.

"I could get used to this pampering very easily. You may be sorry you started something."

"I'll just warn you, I don't do laundry or toilets, otherwise I'm all yours."

They had barely finished eating when Olivia rang the doorbell. "How was your first day, Helen? Did you sell any Hope diamonds?"

"No, but I did hold my own with my co-worker. I didn't short change anyone, and wonder of wonders, my till balanced at the end of my shift."

❦❦❦

Olivia joined her and Gerald for a glass of wine and watched the easy camaraderie between the two. Gerald included her in the conversation and helped to ease Olivia's fear of having intruded. After thirty minutes of conversation, she excused herself and moved toward the door.

"Gotta go, kiddo. I just wondered how the first day went and I'm glad you're enjoying it."

She later related to Sarah during their nightly phone call how she couldn't help the happiness she felt for Helen who seemed to have found a soul mate in this old friend and how she hoped Gerald would fill the void created by that jerk Helen had been married to.

They agreed on how sad it had been to see her brought to her knees emotionally and financially when the dust settled after Edward's death.

"The love affair alone would have been enough to do any woman in, but to have it followed by financial devastation was far more than Helen deserved. I get so worked up every time I think about it. Hopefully this old friendship will help her forget."

❦❦❦

After seeing Olivia out the door, Gerald sat on the ottoman and lifted Helen's feet onto his lap. He started massaging the heel of one foot as he told her to lean back and close her eyes. His fingers were magic and before long she was snoring softly. He kissed the toes of one foot and covered her with a crocheted coverlet. She woke up a short time later to find him wiping down the kitchen counters, everything washed and put away.

She slid her arms around his waist as she came up behind him. After kissing the back of his head she whispered, "Thank you, Gerald, for everything."

He turned and wrapped her in a bear hug. "There's no reason

to thank me. I enjoy looking at your lovely face across the dinner table. It beats staring at the television with a TV dinner on my knees."

"Now I know you're just playing on my sympathy. Stella Jacobson would keep you well fed given half a chance and would gladly share your dining table."

"Stella Jacobson doesn't have your legs."

"You can't see my legs under the table."

"She doesn't have your beautiful, soft, luscious lips." He pressed his own to hers.

"You got me there."

"On the other hand, she does make great biscuits."

"Let's get back to my lips." She leaned into him and moved her lips over his. "I remembered your lips and how they felt. No one ever kissed me quite like you."

"Is that good or bad?"

"Good. Mmm, very, very, good."

He pulled her closer and teased her mouth open just as the phone rang.

"Mom, I've been waiting for you to call and tell me about your first day at work."

"Hi, darling. It went amazingly well." She motioned to the picture of Ellie while she spoke.

Gerald nodded and reached for the sweater he had thrown on the chair by the door. "I'll call you tomorrow," he mouthed as moved toward the door.

"Just a moment, Ellie, a friend of mine is just leaving. I'll be right back."

At the door, she apologized. "I'm sorry, Gerald. Ellie has been so encouraging, I hate to just cut her off."

"I understand. It's time for me to leave and let you relax anyway. Goodnight, brown-eyes." He kissed her again as he went out the door.

"Was that a man's voice I heard?"

Helen took a breath before answering. "Yes, Ellie, it was. An old childhood friend of mine has just moved into the building. I hadn't seen him since we were kids and was pleasantly surprised to have someone I know as a neighbour. He was just checking out my day as well." She plopped on the sofa once again. "Now let me tell you all about this sapphire necklace and earring set I sold to a woman from Japan."

She was relieved an hour later when Ellie hadn't asked any more questions about Gerald. *I'm off the hook for today, but I'm sure it will come up again.* Not really sure how Ellie would take to the idea of her mother having a male friend, Helen decided she would not mention him again unless asked.

On Saturday she was given the third degree by a female customer a few years her senior, who was very interested in knowing all about Helen's job quest. "You mean they called you for an interview just from your resume? You didn't know anyone here to recommend you?"

"I was fortunate enough to follow in the footsteps of a young woman who left to accompany a husband whose career was abundantly more important than hers apparently. The fact that I'm a widow and not attached to anyone whose career might force me to leave was an extremely attractive carrot to place before my new employer's nose."

"So it was being in the right place at the right time, not who you know."

Helen couldn't help but smile. "Yes. I suppose it was. Why are you asking?"

The woman leaned over the counter and whispered conspiratorially, "I'm looking for work as well. My husband had to take an early retirement due to ill health so his pension was adjusted accordingly. We managed okay but when his health took a downturn, we went through our reserves very quickly. He passed away a few months ago and I would really like to add to the small income I'm forced to live on. The company I worked for years ago has computerized and I'm willing to take courses but that doesn't help me in the meantime, nor is it a guarantee that they'll hire me back. I really don't need an executive salary, just enough to help my income stretch to the end of the month."

"Where did you work before?"

"I processed orders for a major candle importer. I used to love walking in the warehouse when new shipments arrived, especially if any crates had been damaged. It was a huge company. If we couldn't get the candle you wanted, believe me, it wasn't made."

"In your position were you required to have in-depth knowledge of the product?"

"Of course. If one word was missing or misspelled in the order, we could end up with a container load of rejected candles sitting in the warehouse."

"So you pretty well knew all the qualities, fragrances, colours, etc." As she was making the statement the woman was nodding her head in agreement.

It was her turn to lean over the counter. "Mrs. …?"

"Dolores, please. Dolores Hoffman."

"Dolores, the day before yesterday when I was walking toward the restaurant, I noticed a candle and bath store down the concourse that had a sign in the window looking for part-time help. Why don't you go down and see if the position is still available then inquire if you can arrange a meeting with the owner. I would advise you to get a resume put together quickly with the emphasis on your experience with candles."

She thought Dolores was going to burst into tears. The woman grabbed her hand and shook it vigorously. After starting towards the door, she turned around and thanked Helen once more. "Remember, Dolores, emphasis your knowledge of candles, not your office experience. They sell high-end merchandise and I'm sure they would appreciate someone who knows the difference between a tea light and a votive. Good luck."

On Monday afternoon, Helen was surprised to see Dolores Hoffman approaching her rather hurriedly. "I start training with the candle shop owner in ten minutes."

"Dolores, that's wonderful. So she was impressed with your resume."

"She hasn't even seen it. I guess my timing was right too. Isabel happened to be in the store the other day after I left here. Another unsatisfied customer had just exited the store when I arrived. I believe she was surprised at first that I was seeking employment but when I told her my history with candles, she hired me on the spot. Apparently, another mother-of-the-bride had been disappointed with the store's service when the wrong length and shade of candles were delivered to the reception hall on Saturday. The fact that I don't have to juggle daycare, babysitters or college classes to fit the schedule clinched the deal. Helen, I don't know how to thank you."

"For what? You did this all by yourself."

"You had the vision to zero in on one little area of my experience and that's exactly what was necessary. Without you sending me in the right direction, I never would have succeeded."

"I hope you enjoy your job as much I do mine. Perhaps we can meet in the court for lunch one day."

That evening when Gerald met her for fish and chips at an English pub nearby, Helen was overcome with a real feeling of satisfaction at having helped a fellow retiree re-enter the workforce. "I wonder how many women like Dolores and me are urgently in need of work and being overlooked because of their ages. There have to be other employers out there who aren't aware of the advantages of hiring an 'age-challenged' woman —

or man, for that matter."

Gerald was amused by the concern in Helen's voice. Her eyes literally gleamed with the passion of an imaginary challenge. "You may have started a new trend, Helen. Other merchants in the mall may see the viability of hiring mature women and soon new doors will be opened to the fifty-plus set."

"Are you making fun of me?"

"Of course not, love. I couldn't be more proud. Not only have you taken charge of your own future, now you've helped another when she was feeling frustration in the same situation. I admire your spirit."

"Dolores and I both found employment in the same building, just by stressing the advantages of hiring women of our age and experience. If more employers were aware of the value women over fifty could bring to their workforce, maybe they would not only consider us, but actively seek us out."

"Perhaps it should be brought to the attention of some of the head-hunting agencies."

"Or an agency set up that specializes in placing women of advanced years."

"Yes, an enterprising individual might consider that a horizon to consider. The research required would be a daunting if not formidable task." The waiter placed their dinners in front of them then set a bowl of fresh cut lemons and a bottle of vinegar in the middle of the table.

After watching Helen toy with the food for several minutes, Gerald rested his fork and knife on his plate. "You are very deep in thought, Helen. What's on your mind?"

She smiled. "Oh, nothing really. I'm just thinking about Dolores and me." She placed a piece of fish in her mouth and sighed. "If I were ten years younger I might give some thought to setting up that agency. Maybe even five years younger …"

# Chapter Six

"Why don't we take the train up to Wakefield in Quebec tomorrow and enjoy some of the scenery along the Gatineau River?" Gerald had been sitting comfortably on his sofa gazing at Helen over his newspaper. "The weather section reports nothing but clear blue skies for the next few days. I've been told there are some very nice restaurants in the town."

"That would be a lovely idea except the train has been out of service for several years."

"Several years? That shows how behind the times I am. Is it closed for good?"

"Some think it is. Others hope someone will supply the necessary funding to get it up and running again. The tracks were washed out a few years ago when the area suffered heavy rains. I understand the cost of rebuilding the track bed is in the millions of dollars. Government funding has been refused so the future of the train is totally dependent on private funding."

Helen had been standing near the window of his comfortable living room. She moved across his elegant, Indian area rug and perched on the giant ottoman in front of Gerald. "It's a beautiful drive if we take the route along the river. Why don't we have a picnic on the grass? Wakefield is a lovely little town with many gift shops and bakeries too. It won't be difficult to find something to put a meal together there or even take out from a restaurant. I would enjoy eating on a bench somewhere beside the river."

Gerald put the newspaper down and took both of her hands

in his. Before he spoke he brought them to his lips and placed a light kiss on each palm. "It sounds wonderful. I look forward to every hour we spend together, Helen. I feel like I've found a treasure I thought I had lost." He gently tugged her arms till she was sitting beside him.

"Why did you go, Gerald?"

"I've asked myself that same question more times than I can count."

"Did you ever come up with an answer?"

"Several. Each one merely emphasizes what a fool I was." His lips were pressed against her temple. "You're wearing a different fragrance today."

"My hair stylist used a new hairspray." She had spent the morning having her hair coloured and her nails manicured. After several days of showing jewellery, she realized that her hands were on display as much as the designs she was holding.

"I like it." He held her chin and lifted her mouth to his. "I like you." He moved away and looked at her apologetically. "I have to leave shortly, Helen. Guy had a cancellation today that frees just enough time to meet me for lunch. This is a rare occasion so of course I jumped at the invitation. I hope you don't mind."

"Gerald, your day doesn't belong to me. I'm delighted you're able to spend some time today with your son. Besides, I have to prepare some wicked snacks. It's my turn for cards today." She started toward the door then turned. "What time do you want to leave tomorrow?"

"I'll call you this evening and we'll decide."

"Okay. Have a nice lunch."

She was late setting up the table for cards. After changing recipes several times, she finally had a dessert cooling in her refrigerator and a frozen quiche from her freezer ready to pop in the oven at the appropriate break time. A tossed salad was all ready, just waiting for dressing. It was a miracle she was able to accomplish all this, plus change her clothes and reapply her make-up after being interrupted with two phone calls.

Dolores Hoffman had called, excitement in her voice. Her employer was so pleased with her knowledge and her sales that she had increased Dolores's hours to twenty-eight per week and given her a five percent increase in wages. "Do you believe it? I've hardly been there a week and already I've received a raise. Helen, I have you to thank for this. Please let me buy you lunch next Saturday."

After assuring her that a reward was not expected, she accepted the offer for lunch when it became apparent that a refusal would hurt Dolores's feelings. Within an hour the phone rang again and it was Helen's own employer asking her to work tomorrow to cover for an ill Jennifer Healey. Remembering her sales pitch for the job with promises of being available whenever needed, she could not very well refuse the first time asked. Gerald would be disappointed but it couldn't be helped. They would just delay their outing by a couple of days because the following day would be Saturday, another work day.

She was setting a couple of small dishes on the table, each filled with bridge mixture and cashews when the doorbell rang. If her friends were ever late for anything it was certainly never for their card games. They always started on time.

Margaret was quick to inform that she did not have Celiac Disease but there was a new doctor in her clinic specializing in diseases of the digestive system so she was quite confident she would be finding a solution to her ailments soon.

"Margaret, I've come to the conclusion that what you need is a good roll in the hay." Olivia was pointing her finger at the stunned Margaret as she spoke.

"Olivia, what a hurtful thing to say. Besides, I don't … I've never …"

"Maybe that's your problem. Maybe you should."

Margaret's face paled behind her stunned expression. It was clear she didn't know what to say. Finally, after her lips moved several times she lifted her chin in a defiant manner and started to whisper "My husband …" then stopped.

"Your husband has been dead for several years. When did your stomach ailments start?"

"Well, it was shortly after he died, but I was distraught. I was upset."

"You were alone and you don't like being alone. You're used to having a man in your life. For the love of God I can't figure out why, but you need one in your life now, Margaret. Guaranteed if you were to meet a nice man and develop a relationship, your stomach disorders would disappear." Olivia patted her hand as she tried to soften the tone of the conversation.

Her friend blushed as she thought about it. "You could be right. I was always in good health when Hugh was alive." She surprised them by continuing, "Maybe I do need to get laid."

They burst into laughter at the sight of poor Margaret struggling to accept that she had just made the last remark.

"Helen, why don't you lend her Gerald for a few weeks, just till we see if her stomach-ache goes away."

"Then she'd probably be replacing her stomach aches with headaches." Helen smiled at Margaret as she spoke.

"Honey, if I had a man like Gerald in my bed, there is no way I would ever have a headache — even if I had one." Sarah joined the conversation. "Margaret, whatever happened to that man on the fifth floor that was phoning you last fall."

"He was swept off his feet by Stella Jacobson's home-made bread. Then he wintered in Arizona and came back with a woman from Edmonton who replaced Stella's buns with her own. Next thing you know, both of them are gone and his condominium is up for sale. I understand they moved to British Columbia somewhere."

"We'll keep our eyes open for you, honey. First single man over fifty that moves into this building is yours." Olivia winked at all of them as she dealt the cards.

It was almost seven o'clock when they called it quits. Before she tidied the kitchen, Helen remembered to call Gerald to cancel their outing for the next day.

"Naturally I'm disappointed, Helen, but I understand. Why don't we still spend half the day together and take a picnic lunch at the Champlain Lookout up in the Gatineau hills? I promise to have you back in time to change for work. I'll even drive you and pick you up again."

Helen laughed. "I have no excuses then, do I? It would be fun." She was just about to hang up then asked, "Can I interest you in a piece of strawberry shortcake? I hate to throw it out and I've already eaten more than I should have. I can have a pot of tea ready in five minutes."

"The garbage can is on his way down, brown-eyes."

"How was your lunch with Guy?"

"Too short. His hour and half was shortened considerably when his blasted cell phone informed him that one of his patients had arrived with a bleeding mouth and half a tooth missing."

"Oh, Gerald, I am so sorry. You were really looking forward to it."

"It seems I'm doomed to the back seat by the careers of those I want to see most."

She didn't see sarcasm in his eyes but thought some might be present in his voice.

"I'm sorry." He lifted her hand to his mouth and kissed her palm. "I must sound like a whiny baby. I don't mean to." His eyes warmed as he asked about the bridge game. "Any new gossip?"

"Not really. Olivia is going to help Margaret find a new husband. They've decided that the lack of a man is the cause of all Margaret's stomach problems."

Gerald looked at her incredulously for a moment before bursting into laughter. After a moment's hesitation Helen joined him.

"Are they going to advertise on the bulletin board downstairs? How does someone arbitrarily go on the hunt for a new husband?"

"Margaret isn't into the bar scene so I don't think they'll start there. She does love bowling so perhaps joining a mixed league might be one answer. When her husband was alive they belonged to a curling club. That might be another place to try. Barring that, there's always the library and church."

"I wish her luck. She's a pretty nice looking woman, she shouldn't find it too difficult."

"After her husband died, she was very lonely. If it hadn't been for us, I think she would have had a hard time coping. Some women really find it hard being alone at night."

"Some men too."

Startled, she lifted her eyes to his. "It seems to get easier with time."

"I guess some need more time than others." He took his teacup to the counter and poured a refill. "There's a documentary on television about ships that have gone down in the Great Lakes. Would you be interested?"

"Yes. Yes, I would. Were any of them boats that you've been on?"

"No, but I did know some crew members on a few of them."

She poured a fresh cup for herself and joined him on the chesterfield. The program was made all the more interesting because he brought it to life for her. His additions to the dialogue and personal experiences were more exciting than the show itself. She could sense his love for the water. "You enjoyed your career, Gerald."

"That's the one thing I have no regrets about. From my first step onto the first deck, I knew that was what I was meant to do. It's a difficult life. Like a navy sailor, you have no home but the ship beneath you. Poor Simone was alone more than we were together. She raised Guy by herself and never complained."

*Lucky her.* Helen thought. She looked at him in profile. *If I had you coming home to me every month or so, I would have considered myself the luckiest woman alive.*

He turned and saw her intent gaze. Without warning, he swept her into his arms and covered her mouth with his. It was a hard kiss, filled with desperation rather than passion. "I didn't deserve her, Helen. All those nights at sea, God forgive me, but it was you I thought of —not her. I loved you then and I love you now." He kissed her again, more gently this time. "I love you." It was a faint whisper against her ear.

She found herself clinging to him, not wanting to let go. She could feel his heart beating against her breast, his ragged breath against her hair. "Gerald, my love." The words were out before she even thought about them. Her lips sought his this time with her own feeling of desperation.

The ringing of the telephone broke the spell.

"Mom. Hi. It's me. I have to come to Ottawa for a few days on business and I wondered if you wanted company?"

"Of course, Nicholas. You're always welcome. Are you coming by yourself?"

"Yes. I was hoping I could bring Benjamin with me. I thought you might enjoy having him with you for a few days but he has an appointment with an eye specialist that we've been waiting to see forever. You'll have to settle for just me."

"I won't be settling. I'll be excited to have you to myself even for a little while. Why does Benjamin need an eye specialist?"

"We're worried about one eye that keeps getting infected. Nothing serious, we hope, but we just don't want to postpone the appointment."

"When are you arriving?"

"On Sunday evening. I have to leave again on Wednesday morning. I know that only gives us a couple of nights together, but we'll cram every minute into them that we can, just you and me. Promise."

"E-mail me your flight number and I'll be at the airport on Sunday."

"Thanks, Mom. See you then."

# Chapter Seven

"That was your son?"

"Yes. Nicholas is coming on Sunday evening to stay for a few days. He has some business in town."

Gerald pulled her to stand close to him. "I'll have to make myself scarce for a few days."

"I would like you to meet him … and he, you."

"I could pick up some of his words and I got the impression he wanted you to himself."

"I'll spend as much time as possible with him. I'll try to arrange my work schedule around him, but I do want him to know you, to know that you are a part of my life."

"Am I, brown eyes?"

She kissed him softly. "You always have been. We just got detoured."

"I have waited so long for you to tell me that you care."

"I care."

He studied her face. "Your eyes are so dark, it's hard to discern the change in colour, but at this moment, they are so black I could get lost in them. I've missed those eyes. They used to stare at me in the darkness aboard ship." He kissed first one lid, then the other.

She tilted her mouth waiting for his lips to travel down to hers. When they didn't, she opened her eyes. He was smiling. "You used to tilt your mouth like that when you were fourteen, waiting for me to kiss it."

"You rarely did."

"At that age my hormones were racing. It took everything I had to keep myself from ravaging more than your mouth."

"And how are your hormones now?"

"Like a fifteen-year-old's."

"Hmm." She closed her eyes and tilted her mouth once more.

Just as she felt the brush of his lips, the phone rang once more. "You answer that and you're a dead woman."

"If I don't answer it, Olivia will only ring the doorbell next."

"Then let's prevent a murder." He walked to her phone and pleasantly said, "Hello."

Helen could tell there was a hesitation on the other end. "I'm sorry, Gerald. I didn't know Helen had company."

"That's okay, but Helen can't come to the phone right now."

"Is she okay?"

"Aside from a little shortness of breath, she's more than okay."

Helen shook her finger at Gerald and pretended outrage.

"Well, in that case, I'll tell Margaret not to bother her in the morning. She'll probably be sleeping in. Goodnight, Gerald."

"Goodnight, Olivia."

"You know they're going to assume you're spending the night here."

"Then let's not disappoint them."

❣❣❣

"Have you heard from Helen yet today?"

"No."

"Do you think we should phone her? What if she's wondering why we haven't called?"

"She'd be a damn fool to wonder, Margaret. I think we've

been replaced on her security system."

"How much do we really know about this Gerald? Can he be trusted? What if he thinks she's been left a rich widow and he's after her money?"

"Are you kidding? The way he looks at her, it's not her money he's coveting. Besides, he's wearing very expensive clothes and drives a big car. Helen was telling me about the exquisite decorating in his apartment so I think he's comfortable in his own right."

"How can that be? He only worked on a boat for a living." Margaret's concern was increasing.

"Some of those guys who work on international ships make pretty big bucks."

"I would just hate to see her get hurt again."

"She's a big girl, Margaret. I think she knows what she's doing."

"Who's a big girl?" Helen caught the last part of the conversation.

"You are. Margaret's worried that Gerald may be on his way to breaking your heart."

"He did that once already. He knows I won't stand for it a second time. The first time I let him live. If it happens again, I'll aim for his balls … then a few minutes later, his heart."

Olivia smiled. "Is this our gentle Helen talking?"

"Gentle Helen moved out. Heart-on-her-sleeve Helen has moved in. God, I promised myself I wouldn't do this ever again and here I am, fifty-six years old, and head over heels in love. Again. With my childhood sweetheart."

"The man worships you, Helen. Any fool can see that. You've got a lot of good years ahead of you, why shouldn't you be sharing them with someone you love?"

"He's a good man, girls. I can't believe he accidentally wandered back into my life after all these years."

❣❣❣

"You were my mother's china teapot."

"Come again?" Helen was sure she had missed something. She had stopped in to see what time it would be convenient for him to come for dinner on Monday evening so he could meet Nicholas.

"You were too good for me."

Obviously, the reason for his sudden departure many years before had been weighing on his mind. He moved with her and positioned her on the sofa beside him.

"My mother didn't have many nice things, Helen. You know that. Even though she was embarrassed by it sometimes, she never let on. Never complained. You know what our house was like, always spotless. What you didn't notice was the furniture strategically placed to cover the worn spots in the linoleum. Slipcovers camouflaged the worn out fabric of the sofa. Our clothes were well scrubbed and ironed and the collars and cuffs turned to hide the wear. We got by okay due to my mother's gift with a sewing machine, a stove, and her ability to stretch a dollar.

"We never went hungry and we learned to set a proper table. Some of our dishes had little chips and cracks in them but it didn't matter because we never entertained at mealtime anyway. Our teapot had a chip on the spout. It had to be held at just the right angle when pouring or it would dribble all over the saucer and tablecloth."

"Gerald, do you honestly think I would have cared, even if I had noticed these things?" She interrupted, confused by his embarrassment of his mother's humble house, even after all these years. He was right about his mother's housekeeping. Helen used to marvel at the shine on those linoleum floors. The carpeting that covered her parents' home seemed dull by comparison. The Mercier house always smelled like a home, she thought. Furniture polish, something baking in the oven and always a soup or sauce simmering on the stove. "I was always envious of the way your mother was … always there."

He continued as if he hadn't heard her.

"My mother caught me standing on a stool one day reaching for a teapot that she kept on the top shelf in a cupboard. 'That's not for your use, Gerald', she said. When I asked her why we never got to use it, she replied, 'That's meant for company. It's kept out of your reach so it can be brought out on special occasions, for special guests.' I asked why they got to use it when we hardly ever had company. Why she didn't think we were special.

"'Some people deserve to be treated a little more special than others. It's not that they're better than us, they're just meant for finer things. They're just like that teapot. It holds the tea and does the same job as our everyday one, but it's meant for a special purpose. If we use the teapot for every day use, then it loses its uniqueness and becomes just ordinary. We all should have something special in our lives that can be admired without touching and brought out and enjoyed on very rare occasions.'

"I never forgot her words, Helen. When I was old enough and wise enough to know that you were the special teapot in my life, I also had to recognize the fact that you weren't meant for my personal enjoyment. You were meant for finer things but I always felt it was my station in life to look after you, protect you. When we finished school, I knew I had to leave. I had to move on and let you do the same. Several times during the first few years, I picked up the phone to call you. Once I even dialled your number but I hung up before you answered. Later I learned that you had married and moved away. I tried to move on but none of the women I dated were you. Finally, I met Simone and over time appreciated that she was special in her own way. Eventually, I realized I wanted her in my life permanently and we were married. My son, Guy, was born within a year but Simone became diabetic and was advised not to have any more children. She was a devoted wife and an excellent mother. She was *almost* able to help me forget you, but not quite. I always felt a little guilty. A little part of my heart always belonged to my first love. My brown-eyed girl."

Helen couldn't see him clearly through her tears. She stood and slowly wandered back to the window, then stood with her arms crossed staring at the colours of the setting sun reflected in the windows of the buildings outside. She realized now that what she had always thought was puppy love had been something much deeper. How could he have thought she was much better than he was? If that was the case then, now the situation was reversed. He obviously was in a much better financial situation than she. Did that make him better than her? Of course not. How could he have thought her so shallow back then? How could he have thought that she was a … a teapot, for God's sake?

He moved behind her and placed his hands on her shoulders. She turned and faced him with tears making little rivulets through her makeup.

"Damn you, Gerald Mercier! Damn you." She started to pound his chest with her fists. "I am *not* a stupid teapot! How could you …" She fought for a breath. "How could you walk out of my life thinking I was? Did you honestly think because I had a father who gave us a comfortable income that I thought I was better than you? Did you think that little of me? I'm glad I owned a small piece of your heart all these years because you sure as hell tore a chunk out of mine. I couldn't figure out what I had done to make you just walk away. Your mother and your sister didn't offer any answers either. I think they were surprised that you mattered to me at all. Did you never tell them how close we were? I thought they knew we were more than just friends. I thought you walked on water, for God's sake. I knew you were afraid of my dad because he was pretty strict with me but I assumed as soon as we graduated you would start treating me like a girlfriend and asking me out. Instead you didn't even come to the dance. You just left town and never came back. I could only presume that was your intention all along and that you never bothered to inform me. It was many, many months before I could even look over at your house and not burst into tears. Your reason for breaking my heart stinks!" She had his shirt bunched in her fists by this time.

"I loved you." It was barely more than a whisper. If he hadn't been watching her mouth, watching the words form, he may not have even have heard them. "I loved you, Gerald."

"I knew you loved me — like a big brother. I couldn't settle for that, Helen."

"I tried so hard to be the perfect wife for Edward. I always suffered a little niggling of guilt whenever a conversation turned to our childhoods or our high school years. I hated him when I learned he had been cheating on me for so long, but I had to face the truth that I had always held something back. I had never given myself completely to him. I had cheated him too. I'm not a china teapot, Gerald. I'm just a plain old porcelain one with a chipped spout."

He drew her in closer and kissed her forehead. "Helen."

She slid her arms around his neck and brought her lips to his. With the connection of the kiss she felt the wasted years return like a winter storm when the snow dissipates then circles around with a vengeance and smothers everything in sight. Once again the despondency and longing she had suffered after he had left her so alone overwhelmed her. "I have to be alone, Gerald. I need some breathing space. I need some time." She reluctantly removed her arms, slipped her feet into her shoes, hesitated as she took her purse then let herself out without a backward glance.

Helen quickly closed her own door and slid the dead bolt into place. She crossed the room and stood staring again at the city lights below. Things were moving too quickly. Her plans had not included a man in her life. She needed independence — total self-reliance. She had said she would never allow herself to be dependent on a man again. Now here she was. Wavering. Was she that vulnerable? Could she be swayed this easily by a man?

She saw her own reflection in the window. She moved closer looking for the determination in the dark eyes staring back at her. What she saw instead was doubt. Uncertainty.

*What's the matter with you, Helen? This isn't just any man. It's Gerald. You know you love him. You told him so. He will never hurt you the way Edward did. You know that.*

She turned and looked about the room. She loved this room. This whole apartment. It had always been hers. *Never ours. Never, ever ours.* Edward had always been too busy to spend much time here. It had never been a haven for him to come home to at night. When he walked out on her, he took her pride and self-esteem with him. She hadn't known then that he had taken their life savings as well. The one thing he hadn't taken was her home. Her safe haven. Now the walls of this haven were being tested.

*What will you want, Gerald? Will you want me to move into your home? Am I ready to have you move into mine?*

She knew almost immediately the answer was no. She needed time. Time that, hopefully, he would give her. She trusted him but she had also trusted Edward. Both men had walked out on her. Both had left her jilted and wondering why. Gerald had explained his feelings of unworthiness but it just didn't seem enough. She had the odd feeling he was withholding something. She sensed the story he had given her was meant to satisfy but that it wasn't really the truth. If she doubted his honesty, how could she trust his love.

*Time. I need time.*

There was no response to his knock on her door the next day.

He had given her twenty-four hours to "breathe". It bothered him that he had only given her half the story, but there was no way he could ever tell her the rest of it. He had hated having to leave her and hated even more being forced to do so, but he was willing to shoulder all the blame rather than cause her more pain. She had told him she loved him, why then was she not answering her door or taking his calls?

He knew the reason he had given for leaving had made him seem shallow but how could he tell her the whole truth? His story about the teapot seemed trite but it was the best he could come up with on short notice. Besides she was like his mother's special tea pot. The truth would be demeaning to his mother and cast her own father in a bad light. Better she think less of him than have doubts about her father who was not alive to defend himself. Mr. McAllister had made it quite clear that he did not consider the son of a former prostitute a suitable contender for Helen's hand. The fact that his father had somehow left the scene before Gerald had been born didn't add to his status as anything more than a whore's bastard, just like his brother. How that knowledge had fallen into her father's hands Gerald still didn't know. His mother had managed to finally marry and give her husband a daughter, Doreen, only to have him succumb to tuberculosis. She was then left to raise three children on her own. A talent with the sewing machine managed to keep them fed and clothed, and taking in boarders helped with the mortgage payments. As soon as Gerald started receiving regular pay cheques from the steamship company, he made sure his mother and sister were taken care of. He didn't want anyone's father refusing his little sister because she was "unsuitable".

# Chapter Eight

Gerald had just finished his breakfast the following morning when Helen rang his doorbell. His smile upon seeing her made her feel a little chagrined.

"I'm sorry for giving you a hard time, Gerald."

He took her arm and drew her into his condo. After pulling her to him and holding her for several moments, he kissed her forehead and wrapped his arms even tighter around her.

"Would you have been happier never knowing why I left?"

"I would have been happier if you had never left at all."

"Knowing how I felt, can you understand my need to distance myself from you?"

"No. I could understand the need for a conversation but not your disappearance. Did it not occur to you that I didn't care whether your mother had nice things or not?"

"My mother's things have nothing to do with it. The fact that I couldn't give you what you were used to having did. It was clear that you deserved someone with your own financial status, not a labourer on a lake freighter. That's what I had wanted to do with my life, Helen, and there was no way I was going to ask you to sit at home waiting for my rare or seasonal visits to home port."

"This is the first I ever heard of your ambitions. You never gave me any indication that you were not planning on going to university and sharing a future together."

"At that age it was a matter of great pride that all our friends would be going on to higher education while I would be expected to get a job and help contribute to the family finances. I never told anyone that I wouldn't be going to university. It was easier just to let you all think I was than to explain that my mother needed me to provide an income. She was not getting any younger and she couldn't keep up the hard work she was doing.

"I'm sorry, Helen." He held her at arm's length and looked into her eyes. "I am so sorry."

"So am I, Gerald. I wish you would have given me the benefit of the doubt and confided in me. You make me feel like a spoiled snob."

He knew that nothing he could say would make her understand, but he was not about to tell her that it was her father who was the snob. Perhaps not a snob really, just a man looking out for his daughter's interests. However, he had let Gerald know in no uncertain terms what he knew about the young man's parental background and that he would expose both Gerald and his mother if he did not leave town immediately upon finishing high school. And never to contact his daughter.

"I know you're not a snob, Helen. Maybe I needed more backbone as a teenager. I truly felt I wasn't good enough for you, that you deserved better."

"And now?"

"Now, I wouldn't care if either or both of us were paupers. I went almost a life time without you and I'm not going to give you up again."

"Then we need to talk."

He felt there was an ultimatum coming but he was ready to fight to the finish. He was not about to lose her once more.

"Gerald, I really do have a new-found feeling of independence. I love you, but I have to be alone for the sake of my own self-esteem."

He started to interrupt but she cut him off before he could

begin. "I always seemed to do what the men in my life wanted me to do. First, I went to the college that my father chose, and then went to work in a career that he chose for me. When I graduated, he arranged for me to work for a friend of his in the accounting department at the paper mill. It was this man who introduced me to Edward. They had met at the golf course. The man's daughter was married shortly after and he arranged for Edward and me to be seated next to each other at the wedding. My father was delighted when we became engaged and gave his blessing for a quick marriage when Edward was transferred here.

"After a few years, I gave up a successful bookkeeping career to raise our family and follow in the shoes of his friends' wives by socializing and planning fund raisers for the hospital and other charities. I completely gave up my own identity to be 'Edward's wife'."

"Helen, I have absolutely no plans of asking you to give up anything to follow my dreams."

"I think I know that, Gerald, but I must do my own thing for awhile. I allowed myself to be caught in a situation almost beyond my control. I am determined never to be caught penniless or reliant on anyone ever again."

"Do you think I might put you in that position?"

"No, I don't think you would. But I never thought Edward would either."

"You are unfairly painting both Edward and me with the same brush."

"The only thing the same about you and Edward is that you're both male."

"Then why the distrust in me?"

"My distrust isn't in you, Gerald. It's in me. Until I'm totally independent, both financially and emotionally, I must live by myself and fend for myself."

"Live by yourself."

"Live by myself."

"So where does that leave me? Us?"

"It leaves us exactly where we are. I hope that we can carry on a relationship. I do love you and I want to be a part of your life and you a part of mine. However, I can't allow you to interfere with my plans for making myself financially stable and independent. I may have to work more and I hope you won't be offended if I have less time to spend with you."

"Helen, if that's what you want then I'll respect your wishes. However, I do have enough money for us to live comfortably for the rest of our lives and I am jealous of the time you work when we could be together." He tried hard not to smile at the determined look on her face. He really did love her independent nature but it was true that he wanted to spend every waking moment with her. *Damn it, even the unwaking moments should be theirs to share!*

"Gerald, will you be content with my promise not to vanish into thin air the way you did when you set out to make your fortune? I intend to build my little empire right here in Ottawa where we can spend our free time together."

"You sure know how to hit a guy when he's down."

"I just have to find my way like you did, albeit almost forty years later."

"I hope you won't consider it a threat to your independence if I buy dinner sometimes or offer to take us on a vacation once in a while."

"Everything's negotiable." He didn't see the mischief in her eyes.

"Everything …? Helen, you drive a hard bargain but if I have to negotiate then you can bet your sweet little ass that I will. I'm the best damn negotiator you ever came up against."

She laughed as she slid her arms around his waist and planted her lips on his chin. "Oh, I can hardly wait to see what your bargaining tool might be."

He was about to suggest a starting point when she pulled away from him and announced that she had to leave for work and would call him later that evening … or maybe the next morning.

Nicholas arrived on Sunday evening. Helen was able to adjust her schedule to have most meals with him. Gerald joined them for lunch on Tuesday and the two men found enough common interests to keep the conversation flowing with no uncomfortable pauses. When her son gave her a hug at the airport he whispered, "I like Gerald, Mom." With a wink he departed through the doorway into the secured departure area.

❣❣❣

Gerald's relief at her promise of a continued relationship was short-lived however as he saw less and less of her over the next few weeks. If she wasn't working herself, she was busy locating positions for friends or friends of friends who suddenly seemed in need of employment. Helen seemed to have become the self-appointed agency that assisted the over-fifty jobless, be they male or female. Her success rate bloomed and soon she became quite proficient at writing resumés and cover letters. The mall merchant managers were soon familiar with her and soon she discovered she had to expand her horizons. It was one afternoon while she was playing bridge that the topic of charging a fee for her services came up.

"But Helen, why would you continue to do a service for free that other agencies are paid a good commission for?" Olivia waited for a reply.

"Other agencies? What do you mean other *agencies*? I'm not an agency. I'm just helping out a few people who are unsure of their approach after being out of the workforce for a while."

"Honey, you are spending more time on 'helping out a few people' than you are on your paying job."

"I am not."

Sarah interrupted, "You spent a whole day just last week helping that man who was let go from that weekly newspaper. I believe he's not the only one you worked with last week."

"He had promised to help his grandson with his college tuition. He couldn't very well let the lad down after just one year at University of Ottawa. I figured somebody out there could use the man's experience and I was right. He will be producing monthly newsletters for that new chain of chiropractors. When the health food store which operates inside two of the chiropractic clinics learned what he was doing, they offered him a contract as well. Once he has established himself with these two clients, he hopes to expand. It was mostly his doing. All I did was find that first client for him."

"For which you should get paid."

"When I saw how relieved and happy he was, that was payment enough."

Olivia shook her head. "You are too naïve to be in the business world, Helen. You had talked once about a need for an employment agency for the over-fifties and it seems to me like you have already started one. Why don't you put out a shingle and start charging for your time?"

Helen opened her mouth to protest but closed it after a moment's reflection. "Maybe you're right. I think I better give this some more thought. I have no idea what I should even charge. Maybe no one will solicit my services if I start charging them."

"Are you enjoying the process of finding jobs for these people?" Margaret looked at her with concern.

"Yes, I am. It's very satisfying, especially knowing that I was in that same position not very long ago."

"Then, sweetie, you should do some research and decide to make it your full time job."

"Oh, I don't think it would ever be enough to become full

time. I'm sure I'll need to keep my job at the jewellery store."

"Helen, you are currently spending as much time helping others as you are working at the store. If you decided to make a career of it, I'm sure it will blossom in no time."

"I know how to keep a set of books and I've learned that I have a certain knack for selling but I don't have any real business training. I'm not even sure how to go about getting started."

Olivia had been staring out the window but turned now, laying down her cards. "My business degree is yours for the next few months. In the meantime, you register at Algonquin College and take a few night courses in business administration. I think they have a small entrepreneur program that may be more what you need. In the meantime, we'll all get on the phone and ask questions of some of the head hunting agencies and learn all that we can."

"What do you mean 'your business degree is mine'?"

"I'll lend you my brain and business background to help you get started. I'll be your Girl Friday for a few months. Once you're established, you're on your own." When she saw that Helen was about to protest she frowned and added, "If you can help people you don't even know without charging them, then I can help a friend without charging her." She shuffled the cards. "Now did we come to play cards or argue all afternoon?"

By the end of the week fee schedules, sample questionnaires and application forms had been gathered from unsuspecting employment agencies. The women had been busy. Olivia retrieved the necessary government data and requirements from the Internet and Helen had already built a list of possible clients and registered at the college for a summer course starting late the following month.

Gerald had patiently waited for Helen to find time for him. He hoped the frenzied activity might ease once the initial start-up requirements had been dealt with. Any offers of help by him had been refused and he was beginning to feel shut out. Finally, after not having Helen to himself for almost three weeks, he left a message on her answering machine that supper would be on the table at his place at seven that evening and he hoped he would not be eating it alone.

At three minutes before seven his door bell rang. Helen stood outside his door with a bottle of red wine in her hand and a bouquet of roses in the other. "I don't have any appointments until ten-fifteen tomorrow morning."

"And I lied. Supper won't be ready for another hour, so let's get that wine uncorked to allow it to breathe, the roses in water and you into something more comfortable."

"I don't have anything more comfortable to get into."

"Yes, you do."

Later, as she watched Gerald toss the salad, she rubbed her finger around the top of her wine glass and smiled. "You're right. Your bed is very comfortable."

"I'm glad you found it so. I was beginning to worry that you would never experience it."

"I've neglected you, I know. I did however warn you."

"You did, on both counts. I'm a big boy though. I can handle it as long as I know you haven't forgotten me completely."

Her arms went around his waist as he placed the bowl on the dining table. She placed her cheek against his back. "I just don't want Stella's buns replacing mine at your table. I have that fear niggling every time I refuse your invitations."

"So it's the fear of Stella's buns that brought you to my door tonight, not the fact that you missed me."

"Her buns are pretty hard to compete with. They've done in more than one man. Just how strong are you?"

"I'm sure I could have lasted another forty-eight hours, at least."

# Chapter Nine

Within two months, Helen had more clients than she could handle. The corners of her dining room were piled waist high with files. She could no longer offer her apartment for card games as her table was completely taken over by a computer and combination fax machine, scanner and printer. Olivia had offered her services for only a few months but soon found she was extracting as much satisfaction from this business venture as Helen. If business kept increasing at the current rate, she knew her entrepreneurial friend would soon have to expand to larger quarters. When the phone rang, she picked it up and wondered whether Margaret had read her mind. "Olivia, is Helen there?"

"No. She's getting her hair cut this morning."

"Oh. I'll call her on her cell phone. I'm down on Banks Street and I noticed one of my favorite little shops closed. The owner was inside cleaning and I asked her about it. It seems she had to give up her business due to health reasons, but she owns the building and is looking for a tenant. I told her about Helen and she's willing to negotiate a reasonable rent if Helen will take it "as is" and immediately. Since she's in the neighbourhood right now, maybe she can come by and take a look at it."

"This is a real coincidence. I'm working in her crowded dining room and thinking that she's soon going to need larger quarters. Please give her a call and encourage her to drop in to see it before she leaves the area."

It was early afternoon before Helen returned to her apartment. Her excitement showed and when she presented the proposed rental agreement to Olivia, the two agreed that it would be in Helen's best interest to sign on the dotted line. The price was right, the location was excellent and the space was divided into two rooms, one slightly larger than the other. A two piece washroom and air-conditioned comfort were all included. Helen didn't have to twist Olivia's arm to agree to another six month commitment as "Girl Friday".

First thing in the morning she phoned Mrs. Graham to tell her she had a new tenant for the shop space. Helen decided to let her answering machine pick up messages while she and Olivia shopped for second-hand office furniture and arranged for a telephone business line. The larger room in front was chosen as the main reception room and the smaller one in the rear would offer a modicum of privacy and therefore could be used for client interviews when necessary.

Within a week they were up and running at their new location. Olivia had agreed to take a small monthly salary and man the office while Helen pounded the beat for jobs for their clients. It wasn't long before the move to professional quarters paid off. A small advertisement in the Ottawa Citizen led to an interview with one of the morning news shows and before they knew it, a part-time receptionist was needed to give both ladies some time off during the day.

December was approaching and stores required additional sales help and delivery persons for the holiday season. Helen tried to limit their business hours between ten and four daily but soon found herself in the office at nine in the morning and sometimes staying till six in the evening. Gerald dragged her out for lunch some days and several times a week he cooked dinner for her. The number of times she cancelled at the last minute were increasing and many times she was out on a call when he stopped by at lunch time. Soon the meals they shared became less and less frequent and evenings out were non-existent. After being on the go all day, Helen found she just wanted to stay in and unwind. She had long since given up her job in the jewellery store —one of her clients was happy to take it over.

It was the first week in December and there was still no snow on the ground. Olivia and Kate, the receptionist, had decorated the office with a little artificial Christmas tree. They were in the process of hanging lights inside the large front window while Helen stood on the sidewalk smiling at the warmth the office exuded. The office décor was simple but welcoming. It was late afternoon on an overcast day and the Christmas lights were glowing brightly.

"Your office looks very nice, Helen. I understand you're very busy."

Helen turned to see Stella Jacobson walking toward her. "Thank you, Stella. Yes, we're doing quite well, especially with the busy Christmas selling season."

The two women watched the other two finishing the window decorations for a moment.

"Would you like to come in and have some apple cider with us, Stella?"

"Maybe another time, thank you. I have to get home and dress for a concert tonight. I was at the hairdresser's down the street and just wanted to peek in your window. I'd heard you had a very nice office and that you and Olivia are kept pretty busy."

"Oh. Well, stop by anytime you are in the neighbourhood. What concert are you going to?"

"Gerald Mercier is taking me to dinner and the first Christmas concert at the National Arts Centre this evening. It's he who has been telling me all about your successful business, Helen." She looked at her watch then waved as she turned and walked to the car park a few doors down the street.

# Chapter Ten

"The bitch!"

"Olivia, I guess I can't really blame Gerald. I've not been available too much lately."

"Helen, you've not been available at all. If a man like Gerald was interested in me, there is no way I'd give Stella Jacobson an opportunity to make a move on him." Margaret scolded with her forefinger.

"I had hoped he might be a little more understanding."

"Understanding of what? That you work every single day and then are too tired to see him at night? Do you expect the man to become a hermit because you have to make a living?"

"Margaret, give me a little consideration here. I do have to make a living and Gerald knows it. He said he would be there for me."

Olivia looked at her for a long moment. "You don't, you know."

"I don't what?"

"Need to make a living".

"How am I supposed to pay for my condo and my groceries?"

Sarah joined the conversation. "It seems to me the man has made it quite clear he wants to marry you and look after you till death do you part."

"Oh, no. No. I will not go that route again. I'm just getting to the point where I'm managing to put a little nest egg away. Once the Christmas rush is over, things should slow down a little and I'll have more time for a love life."

"Are you kidding? All those people you found jobs for will be laid off and back in your office hoping you will find some new employment for them." Olivia always saw the business from every angle.

"Maybe by then your love life won't have time for you." Margaret actually looked sad.

"Well, I can't deal with this right now. If Gerald loves me the way he says he does, then he'll have to understand my situation and deal with it."

"Helen, it appears that he is dealing with it … with Stella's help."

"I don't want to hear anymore about this tonight. I'm tired and I'm going to my apartment and to bed. The office is closed now for the weekend and I intend to relax for two days."

She quickly left Sarah's apartment and couldn't wait to get to the seclusion of her own. After a relaxing bath and watching the news in bed, Helen turned out the lights and rolled on to her side, hopefully to have a full night's sleep. Her imagination kept stirring up images of Gerald and Stella at the NAC, lingering over wine after their dinner, and then holding hands while watching the concert. After tossing and turning for several hours, she got up and warmed a glass of milk. Her eyes became moist with unshed tears. *I'll bet Stella wouldn't think twice about letting Gerald support her so why am I having such a hard time with it. He loves me. He'll wait.* She saw her reflection in the glass door of the microwave and held up her warm milk in a mock toast. *Who am I kidding? She's out with him tonight and I'm home alone, unable to sleep.* She finally gave up arguing with herself and dumped the remaining half glass of warm milk down the sink, climbed back into bed and pulled the covers over her head.

❣❣❣

"Do you think someone should tell her?" Margaret asked.

"Are you volunteering for the job?" Olivia looked at Margaret as she asked.

"No, of course not. I just think one of us should tell her before Stella does."

"There's that. I just don't think any one of us has the stomach to break her heart."

"Well, you can bet, Stella will and not think twice about it. I just can't believe that Gerald can be that fickle. Do you really think they're sleeping together?"

"When he leaves Stella's apartment at seven o'clock the morning after a big date with her the night before, I don't think he got up early and went to her apartment to share a piece of toast with her. Guaranteed he enjoyed a sleep-over."

"The bastard!"

The two friends wouldn't have known about Gerald leaving Stella's apartment if Margaret hadn't checked on a cat belonging to a neighbour who was away for the weekend. She had just opened the door to leave the cat owner's condo when she heard Stella's door open and saw Gerald emerge and walk to the elevator. It upset her so completely that she immediately woke Olivia up to share what she'd just seen.

❣❣❣

Helen, unaware of her friends' quandary, innocently slept in after tossing and turning most of the night. When she finally awoke around mid-morning, it was to the sound of her phone ringing.

"Hi, Mom. Did I wake you?"

"That's okay, Ellie. It's time I was up anyway."

"You're not usually a late sleeper. Are you not feeling well?"

"I'm fine. I stayed up a little late last night and after a busy week, I guess I just needed to saw a few extra logs this morning."

"Well, I'm glad I caught you. I was afraid you might have already gone into your office."

"I shut it down for the weekend, Ellie. Five days a week is enough. My friends already think I'm a slave to it."

"I hope you're going to keep it shut down for awhile over the Christmas holidays, Mom. Willis and I would like you to come to Kingston and enjoy the holiday with us."

"Oh, sweetie, I haven't even thought about my plans for Christmas yet."

"Good, then you don't have any and therefore no excuse not to come here. We're hoping you can come Christmas Eve and stay through Boxing Day."

"Well, I certainly will give it serious thought. How are Melanie and Andy?"

"Great. They're already making their lists for Santa Claus."

"Will Santa share those lists with me?"

"He'd be more than happy to, I'm sure. So what are you going to do with your weekend? Do you and Gerald have any plans? I noticed there's a great Christmas concert running at the National Arts Centre right now."

Helen hesitated momentarily. "I think I'm going to take the weekend to decorate my condo for Christmas. After being out all week, I want to stay close to home. My business is going great guns and if it continues, I may hire more help. I'm not used to being gone from morning till night and it is tiring. I thought I might have a slow-down after the holidays but Olivia seems to think it may get even busier. So I don't want to tire myself too much."

"Gee, Mom, I hope you're not overdoing it. I would hate to see you get run down. Please consider coming to stay with us over the holidays and let us pamper you a little."

"I promise I'll give it serious thought, Ellie. I should shower and dress now before any of my neighbours decide to pop in for coffee. I'll call you soon and let you know about Christmas."

She no sooner hung up the phone when it rang again.

"Helen, it's Gerald. Can I stop in for a cup of coffee? There's something I want to talk to you about."

# Chapter Eleven

Helen asked for an hour to shower and dress, to which Gerald reluctantly agreed. What else could he want to talk to her about except the fact he was now seeing Stella. His honest nature was coming through in that he must feel compelled to tell her rather than ease out of their relationship without a word.

She had just stepped out of the shower when her phone rang. Wrapping a towel around her wet body, Helen quickly strode into her bedroom to answer.

"Hello."

"Helen, I'm glad I caught you in."

"Olivia, I don't have time to chat right now. Gerald will be here in less than forty-five minutes and I just stepped out of the shower."

"Gerald is coming up? What does he want?"

"I'm not sure. Apparently, there's something he has to talk to me about. Maybe, his conscience is bothering him about Stella."

"Oh, so you know then."

"Know what?"

Olivia realized that she may have spoken out of turn and maybe Helen wasn't aware of Gerald's latest sleeping arrangement. "Oh, um, about him dating Stella."

"Olivia, I was the one to give you that message. I don't think that's what you had on your mind. What gives?"

"Nothing, I guess I'm confused about what I'm hearing from whom?"

"Give it up, Olivia. You never get confused about anything. You have something else you're not telling me."

"It's nothing really. You better go and get ready for Gerald. I'll call you later."

"You'll tell me now before he gets here. What is it, Olivia? If there's something more than a date, I would like to be prepared for it."

"Well, oh dear, this is so difficult and it could really be nothing."

"What?"

"This morning Margaret saw Gerald leaving Stella's apartment very early, with a little duffle bag in his hand."

"Duffle bag? As in overnight things duffle bag?"

"Yes. Helen, I'm so sorry."

"Well, I guess it was bound to happen, wasn't it? You did warn me, didn't you?"

"Now, Helen, it may not be what it seems. You have to hear what Gerald has to say."

"No, Olivia, I don't. This will be the second time in my life that he has deserted me. I will not stand for it. I'm not sure I even want to hear his excuse. Of course, it will be all my fault."

"I wouldn't say *all* your fault … exactly."

"You're sticking up for the bastard. He can't give me some space for a little while without running to the first available female? That's it! I'm done with men, once and for all. Gerald Mercier can go jump in the lake. I'm not opening my door to him."

"Helen, don't do anything hasty. Let him at least …" Dial tone.

Helen quickly dried her hair, dressed and applied some make-up. A glance at her watch told her she still had twenty minutes before Gerald would be at her door. She grabbed her purse, threw on her coat and let herself out. She took the elevator right down to the parking level and quickly drove away from the building.

*Maybe, I'm being a coward but I can't face him. How could he have slept with Stella? Taking her out for an evening is one thing but sleeping with her crossed a line. You bastard, Gerald. I let you into my heart and you break it again. No more. No more, do you hear me? I will not be trod on again.*

The tears were making it hard to see where she was driving. It really didn't matter because she had no idea where she was going. After driving around aimlessly for more than an hour, Helen realized she was in the west end of town. She pulled into the Bayshore Shopping Mall parking lot and shut her engine off. After sitting and crying for a few minutes, she pounded the steering wheel with her fists. The sobs came like a burst dam.

A tapping on her window drew her attention. She looked up to see a young man with a concerned look on his face. "Are you all right, Ma'am? Do you need help?"

Helen drew a couple of deep breaths and shook her head. She opened her window a couple of inches. "I'm fine. I just got some bad news and it finally hit me. Thank you."

She started her car again. Not quite ready to go home yet, and afraid to go to the shop in case someone came looking for her there, she considered what her alternatives were. Trying to think where she could lay low for the rest of the afternoon and not have to actually see people or be seen, she remembered a movie cinema in the west end. Perfect place to hide. A quick check of the damage to her face showed only her eyes were in need of repair. A wipe with a tissue and fresh mascara took care of most of it and she was ready to go.

After the movie, Helen went to a nearby donut shop and ordered a bowl of soup and a bagel. She had already forgotten the name of the movie and had no recollection of what it was about. All she'd been able to think about was the pain. The pain of being jilted for another woman — again. The pain of realizing that

Gerald, who really did own her heart, had walked out of her life — again. The pain of knowing she could trust absolutely no man again. By this time it was late afternoon and she felt it might be safe to go home. Gerald would have the message by now.

When she let herself into her apartment, she noticed the message light blinking on her phone. "Keep right on blinking. I'm not in a returning-messages mood." Her cell phone was still sitting on the charger where she had placed it the night before. "I'm not checking you either."

After downing a whole pot of tea and watching the six o'clock news, Helen called her daughter to accept her Christmas invitation. A glance at the clock told her she could still make the evening mass at her church nearby. She had not attended in several months but suddenly felt she needed the comfort and refuge that it offered.

It was a little chilly for walking so once again she drove her car out of the parking garage and headed a few blocks west. The church was warm and the choir was warming up before mass. She always loved listening to the hymns, especially during advent and Christmas. Deep in prayer, she caught the movement of someone moving into the pew beside her. As she moved to make room, she caught a familiar scent.

"Hello, Helen. I'm surprised and grateful to finally catch up with you."

# Chapter Twelve

"Gerald, I …" She couldn't finish the sentence as she looked into those dark brown eyes, now appearing to smoke with the intensity of his glare.

"Not now, Helen." He took her hand in his. "But we are going to talk before this evening is over."

She withdrew her hand and tried to put some distance between them but someone else slid into the pew and they were squeezed together once more. Her heart was pounding at the closeness of him. The tears were too near the surface for comfort. She glanced around but of course there was no escape short of just getting up and leaving. She bowed her head. *Dear God, I came to you for comfort and you bring me Gerald. Why are you playing games with me? It's not fair. Or maybe … Oh no, please don't let the reason Gerald is here is because Stella Jacobson is a member of the choir.*

Her senses were swimming from his cologne. The nearness of him was too much to bear. If he turned those eyes on her one more time she just knew she was going to fall apart. The homily slid right by. She heard it but nothing registered. The priest could have been talking about a seat sale on one way tickets to heaven for all she knew. The collection plate was passed then they were standing reciting the Lord's Prayer. When it came time for the sign of peace, instead of the usual handshake, Gerald held her shoulders and placed a kiss on her cheek. She was ready to explode. *I can't stand this. I can't bear to have him close like this and know that his heart is with someone else. I have to get out of here without him. I can't endure having him tell me it's over between us, that he'll be spending his evenings and nights with Stella now.*

Looking around for an escape route, it finally came. As everyone started to leave the pew to proceed to the front of the church for communion, Helen remained in her seat and let Gerald slip by her to join the line. Once he was in the main aisle on his way to the front, she picked up her purse and headed to the back of the church. Relieved to be crossing the parking lot and with her key in her hand, she was just about to punch the car opener when she felt a hand slide inside her arm and take a firm grip.

"You are not getting away that easy."

"What the …?"

"Lucky for me, I turned just in time to see you leave the pew, Helen."

"Take your hands off me."

"Not on your life. Now, open your car door."

"I will not."

"Fine, we will stand out here in the cold and have our conversation."

Just then a gust of wind swirled through the parking lot and blew some snow off the roof of the car right into her face.

"Helen, we really would be more comfortable inside. Why don't we go for a drink or a bite to eat? Have you had dinner yet?"

"I'm not going anywhere with you, Gerald. Not now. Not ever again."

"Suit yourself, but you will hear me out, Helen."

She stiffened her spine in defiance but could not summon the courage to look at him. He put an arm around her shoulders and tried to draw her closer. When he put a finger under her chin to draw her face up, she shook him off and turned her back to him.

"You're acting like you're ten years old again."

"I wish I was ten years old again. I would know better than to give my heart to a … a … scoundrel who would only break it again and again."

"Scoundrel? Helen, I …"

"Excuse me. I need some room to open my door." The owner of the car next to Helen's was trying to get by them to access his car.

"Sorry." Gerald eased Helen ahead a bit.

As the car backed away they were aware of more people making their way to their vehicles. A couple of women called out to Helen and waved. One, an acquaintance from the mall where Helen had worked came over to ask about her new business and waited for an introduction to Gerald. After a brief conversation, Helen realized she was not going to get rid of Gerald that easily.

"All right, I'll open the car but I will not go anywhere with you."

Gerald moved around to the passenger door and slid inside before she changed her mind.

Helen started the motor and adjusted the dials to defrost the windshield and to get some interior heat. Gerald turned and leaned against the door, looking directly at her.

"Why did you leave your apartment after agreeing to see me this morning?"

"I agreed to see you before I knew the whole story of your previous twelve hours."

"Which was what exactly?"

"Gerald, don't play games with me. I know where you were all night and I really don't want to hear your version of it. I … I couldn't bear it. Now if you will get out of my car, I would like to go home."

"How do you know where I was all night?"

"I know you had a date with Stella Jacobson last night and

then you were seen tip-toeing out of her apartment in the early morning hours."

He raised an eyebrow at that and shifted in his seat.

"And you took that to mean what, Helen?"

"I took it to mean exactly what it was, Gerald. I'm not stupid nor am I naïve. I'm also not into playing musical beds with any man. So that's it. You want Stella, you got her. No contest. I don't need to hear explanations or confessions or apologies if that's what you're about. I have a busy life and I'll get over you."

"So based on that, it's just so long Gerald? No explanations required?"

"That's right. I don't have time for games. Now, out of my car, out of my life. I'll see you around."

"I can't believe you would write me off that easily, Helen."

"I have news for you, fella. You are written off — not easily, granted, but written off just the same. Now unless you want to ride back in this car and have to walk back for yours, I would advise you to get out, now."

Gerald placed a hand on her arm as she reached to shift gears. He waited for her to look at him. Were his eyes really moist?

"If you ever decide you want to finish this conversation, I will be more than happy to do so, Helen."

He exited the car and dragged his feet toward the lone vehicle at the other end of the parking lot.

# Chapter Thirteen

Helen buried herself in her work. As Christmas drew near, it seemed to ease as most of her potential clients had work to keep them busy through the holidays. It appeared that no one was thinking beyond that point. She caught glimpses of Gerald coming and going around the building but for the most part, she buried herself in her work and tried to rest in between. Her friends told her that Gerald and Stella seemed to be an item. When the condo owners had a reception in the common room that was timed to include holiday celebrations of different faiths, Helen chose not to go. Apparently, Stella was playing the role of hostess and Gerald seemed quite happy to be by her side.

Helen's heart was breaking but she was determined to get over it. She busied herself with shopping for her grandchildren and finalizing plans for her visit to Kingston over Christmas.

The Friday before Christmas week, Helen closed her office until the Monday after New Year's which gave her two full weeks to relax and recharge. She had confirmed with Ellie that she would arrive during the afternoon the day before Christmas and stay through Boxing Day, maybe even the day after.

Through the grapevine she heard that Stella was going to her son's home in Windsor for the holidays and Gerald was going skiing with his son in New Hampshire for several days over Christmas.

Olivia was heading to Florida for a month so Margaret and

Sarah decided to blow the budget and made a reservation for Christmas dinner at Chateau Laurier.

It was the evening of December twenty-third, when Helen's doorbell rang. Expecting a delivery of poinsettias from the florist, she opened it without checking her peephole. After flinging the door wide, she was confronted with a smiling Gerald carrying a gift-wrapped parcel.

"Hello, Helen. May I come in?"

"I . . . I . . ."

"I'll take that as a yes." He sailed right by her and continued into her living room.

"I didn't say yes."

"But you didn't say no either."

"What do you want, Gerald? I'm rather busy."

"That seems to be the story of your life right now. Always busy."

"Some of us have to work for a living."

"That's not entirely true now, is it Helen." It was a statement rather than a question.

"I don't know what you mean."

"I offered you a life without working. I offered to share my life with you."

"You know why I couldn't do that, Gerald. I thought you understood."

"Are you on your way to achieving your goal, Helen? Are you nearing financial independence?"

"I don't think that's any of your business."

"I want it to be my business. I want you to be my business."

"What's the matter, did Stella cut you off? I'm sure it will pass." She knew as soon as she said it she had gone too far. The dark eyes and the raised eyebrows told her she had overstepped her bounds.

"Stella Jacobson has no reason to cut me off."

"Then why are you here, Gerald? I told you I'm not into sharing."

"Neither am I, Helen. Neither am I. I was foolish enough to think I could be the most important thing in your life but I was mistaken. I had hoped I could be your reason for getting out of bed everyday and your reason for living. I was wrong. I'm not your most important passion and, frankly, I'm tired of playing second fiddle. I waited hoping that you would come to love me more, but as I said I was wrong. I won't bother you again. I sincerely hope you have a nice Christmas, Helen."

When the door closed solidly behind him, Helen finally let her breath out in a long whoosh. *What was that all about?* She stood in silence listening to her grandfather clock tick away the minutes. He had left the parcel he came in with. It sat on her coffee table. Was it meant for her? Had someone given it to him and he happened to still have it with him when he decided to visit her? What if Stella had given it to him? If that was the case, he would be back for it, otherwise she would ignore it.

The time neared for her to leave for Ellie's. She had decided to take the train down and it would soon be time to call a taxi to take her to the station. The parcel Gerald had brought the day before was drawing her attention. Should she take it up to him? Surely if he had wanted it, he would have come for it. Maybe not. Maybe he really didn't want anything more to do with her.

Margaret and Sarah had been by earlier to exchange gifts with her and to wish her a happy holiday with her family. She had not told anyone about Gerald's visit the day before. She had been somewhat confused by his conversation. Did he think she had another man in her life? He had said he was not into sharing either. Who did he think he was sharing her with? There was no one she would rather be with than him. She wanted to be with him even now. It was only pride keeping her from going to him. Damn it, she did have her pride. Did he think he could sleep with

Stella whenever he wanted and that she'd be sitting there waiting for him? She waited for no man. She had once and would never be so foolish again. Gerald knew that. He knew she had been stung and was determined to make her own way. Passion indeed. She needed another passion like she needed a hole in her head. The only passion she had was her need to build a financial cushion for herself.

She checked her taps and thermostat and called for a taxi. Her things were all loaded on the luggage cart the tenants shared and as she let herself out the door, the last thing she saw was the gaily wrapped parcel sitting on her coffee table.

# Chapter Fourteen

Helen was awakened on Christmas morning by two children bouncing on her bed. "Wake up, Grandma. It's almost lunch time."

The clock beside her bed told her this was not true, it was only eight o'clock. "Lunch time, hmm? I don't think so."

"Mom won't let us open our presents until you're up. Please, can you get up now? Please, please?" Melanie's face was inches from hers and she was holding one of her grandmother's eyes open to make sure she didn't go back to sleep.

"Okay. I'll tell you what, you go and ask your mother to get a cup of coffee ready for me and I'll make a quick trip to the bathroom."

"Hooray. She's getting up, Mom." Andy shouted as he ran out her bedroom door and down the hallway.

Helen took the time to wash her face and brush her teeth before she ventured into the living room.

The Santa gifts had already been opened and played with but all the others under the tree were still in their bright wrappers. Five-year-old Melanie was sitting on one end of the chesterfield waiting. "Come sit by me, Grandma." She patted the cushion beside her.

By nine, all the presents were opened and the smell of cooking bacon wafted from the kitchen. Helen was delighted with the heavy button-front sweater that would see her through spring. It would match a number of her pants and one of her skirts. Santa Claus had brought her an IPOD as well, loaded with all her favourite music.

Helen's thoughts kept turning to Gerald as she sat at the kitchen table and picked at the food on the plate in front of her. Was he having breakfast this morning with Stella? She knew he was leaving later in the day for a skiing vacation with his son. Was he thinking of her at all? Earlier in the fall they had talked of taking a Christmas vacation together. How had things gone so terribly wrong? *Just like a man! Through my own hard work, I'm finally becoming financially secure and the man I love takes a hike. Selfish. That's what he is. Well, he can have Stella's damn buns—figuratively and literally.*

She was having difficulty holding back the tears. He should have been/could have been beside her this morning. Had she been the selfish one? She had told him her goal was financial independence. Time was running out. No longer in her twenties or thirties, she had only a few years to get it done. How had the time he had been spending with Stella gone unnoticed until it was too late? Was it too late? She remembered the dark moist eyes that had looked into hers in the church parking lot.

"What's wrong, Mom? Mom?"

"Hmm, dear? Did you say something?"

"I asked if something is wrong." Ellie had been watching her mother poke at the soft yokes of her eggs until they had cooled to a soft, sickly yellow gel. She stood and reached for Helen's plate. "It doesn't look like you're going to eat this. What's bothering you, Mom?"

"Nothing."

"Don't tell me nothing. You haven't been yourself since you got here. I'm worried that your business is sapping the energy from you. I don't hear you talk about Gerald anymore. I'll bet you don't even play bridge with your friends as much as you used to.

It seems like you've stopped living, Mom."

"I'm sorry, sweetie. Christmas always makes me a little melancholy, thinking about the great times we had when you were young." She lied as she realized Ellie had hit close to the truth. It wasn't her melancholy that was overtaking her enjoyment of the holiday with her family it was her loss of Gerald.

"We did have some great ones, didn't we?" Ellie continued into some remembered times when she and her brother had created havoc during the opening of their gifts, the fun they'd had with the outdoor sports they shared as a family during the school break. Helen ended up laughing profoundly and her mood passed. She had a little lighter heart as she dressed for Mass.

After dinner, when the dishes from the turkey dinner were done and the kitchen all cleaned, the family settled in the comfy great room to watch one of the movies downloaded for this occasion. Helen soon found her mind wandering again and a depression settled over her. Realizing she had missed a good portion of the movie while lost in her own thoughts, she mentally tried once again to shake her mood. She smiled at the sight of her family gathered around her and wondered what could be more perfect than that. *You should be ashamed of yourself, Helen Whittaker. Look how blessed you are. Do you know how many people have no one to share the holidays with?*

That night she dreamt of Gerald. It was brief and consisted of nothing more than being separated from him by a fog. He was trying to reach her but the fog seemed to make them drift farther apart. Every once in a while she could hear him calling — something about losing her passion. When she finally broke through the mist, it wasn't Gerald on the other side but Stella Jacobson.

Helen woke up with a start to find the sun already lighting her room. Once again a melancholy embraced her and her thoughts turned to Gerald. She did love him. She knew that. It was her love for him that made their separation so painful. Her pillow was damp from her tears, when she forced her sluggish body out bed. A refreshing shower enabled her to join her family with a reasonable facsimile of a happy smile on her face.

They went tobogganing on some nearby hills and she thoroughly enjoyed the fresh air. Phone calls had been exchanged the day before with Nicholas and his family. It had been great sharing the holiday with all her grandchildren, in person and by Skype. She admitted to herself that she really was more tired than she had realized.

A really nice start to her nest egg had been compiled over the past few months. After paying all her expenses, she was pleased to see that she had enough left at the end of each month to add to her meagre investment portfolio. Were the sacrifices she'd made to personal life worth it? It would be nice to slow down a little bit, enjoy some leisure, but, and it was a giant BUT, she knew if she was to reach her goal she had to continue to apply herself. One more year might make the difference. She would have to sit down when she got home and take another look at her finances. She was quite certain she might be about a year ahead of schedule if she was counting right. Tonight belonged to her family so she would postpone worrying about finances until tomorrow.

Fortunately, the railway had been able to accommodate her change of plans when she let her family talk her into staying the extra day so they could all enjoy attending a Kingston Frontenacs hockey game. She was glad she had stayed. It gave her more time to relax and not think about her situation in Ottawa. Willis had her things loaded in the back of his SUV two hours before train time. They had decided they would grab a late lunch downtown before going to the station. The day was a mix of freezing rain and wet snow. It was forecast to deteriorate even more as the day progressed. She was glad to be heading home. Hopefully the weather was better further north and east, away from Lake Ontario and the St. Lawrence River. By the time she was on board the train, the streets were becoming slippery and her family was anxious to get home. The darkening skies made mid-afternoon feel like early evening.

Helen settled into her seat and as the train pulled away from the platform and her waving family was out of sight, she pulled a magazine from her bag. Determined that the weather was the cause of her funk, she tried to concentrate on one of the articles in the magazine. It wasn't long before she was staring out the window, Gerald once more on her mind. Damn the man. She was determined to put him behind her and to get on with her life but those deep brown eyes seemed to be gazing back at her from the window. His accusation of her having another man in her life kept niggling at her. Gerald had referred to "her passion". He said he wasn't into sharing either. Did he think she had a lover? Who did he think this might be? Where would he get such an idea from? Stella? Would Stella be spreading rumours? She laughed as she reminded herself that the only other passion in her life was her business.

*Oh, my goodness. That's what he's talking about? He's jealous of my business!* It couldn't be possible. He had been very supportive of her, at least in the beginning. What had changed? When had it changed? The realization dawned. It had changed when she had gotten so busy that she had no time for him. How many times had she refused dinner with him? Been too busy to break for lunch with him? How often had she come home in the evening too tired to even see him? How many times had he left her office disappointed because she couldn't even join him for coffee? *Helen, you are a fool. You could have had both, Gerald and a career, but you got greedy. No, not greedy exactly, overzealous maybe. Caught up in the whirlwind of success.* Her eyes were dampened by tears once again, knowing she had lost the one thing that would have made her life complete. He had wanted to be her reason for living, her reason for getting up in the morning. She had been blinded by her ambition to be independent. *Gerald what have I done?*

As the train sped along, the weather was closing in, adding to her depression. They left the main track at Brockville and started north. The wet snow had turned completely to ice and sleet, making beautiful, impenetrable configurations on the windows. Even with the lights on inside their car, it was dark and gloomy.

She remembered the little parcel on her coffee table. All of a sudden she wanted to get home, to open it. She would call Gerald to see if it was too late for them.

*"I'm on my way home, my love. I will do whatever it takes to get you back! I love you more than life itself."*

No, she would text him. Those are the exact words she would tell him. When she took out her cell phone it showed there was no connectivity.

Just then the lights went off in the train and as Helen was thrown against the seat in front of her she heard the ear piercing sounds of metal scraping on metal.

# Chapter Fifteen

Gerald felt the clouds closing in on them. The skiing had been great but the runs and lifts now were shut down because there was a front moving in from the west. They had hoped for one more day together. With Guy building his practice they didn't get much time to hang out together. Besides what did he have to rush home to? An empty apartment? Stella Jacobson? He'd had enough pies, muffins and fresh baked bread to last him a lifetime.

God, how he missed Helen. If she would only give an inch, he would offer her a mile. That bastard of a husband of hers must have been a real piece of work. Gerald hated to see her working so hard just to make ends meet. Didn't she know? Couldn't she see that it didn't matter to him what she had? He just wanted to take care of her, cherish her for the rest of their lives. Maybe he had given up too easily. She had made him so angry the way she jumped to conclusions. She had him and Stella in bed and practically married. He didn't want anybody in bed with him but Helen. The more he thought about her, the quicker he wanted to get home and take her in his arms. He was not taking no for answer this time. If she wouldn't marry him, he would insist that she move in with him. At least then he would see her first thing in the morning and last thing at night.

The sky was getting pretty dark and the snow had started. If they could just make Montreal by mid-afternoon then they'd be home by dinner time the latest. The highway between Montreal and Ottawa was a pretty easy drive, not too many hills or curves. He would phone Helen as soon as he got home. No, he decided, he would not phone and give her another opportunity to slip away. *I'll use the key you gave me, Helen. I'll bet you forgot all about it. A locked door won't keep me from you. Before this day is finished, you will know once and for all what it means to be truly loved, brown-eyes.*

When the vehicle swerved slightly, it brought Gerald out of his reverie. A look outside told him the weather was deteriorating.

"Are you okay to drive, Guy?"

"Yes. I changed to four wheel drive a little while ago. The slush on the highway is thickening and forming ruts that keep pulling me over. As long as I hold the wheel tight and stay near the centre of the road, I can keep it straight. We aren't far from Montreal and the driving should improve a little. You've been quiet, Dad. Did you doze off?"

"Not really, just kind of day dreaming."

"Oh? What about?"

"Nothing really." He was hesitant to talk to his son about his love life — or lack thereof.

"I couldn't help but notice you've been a little pensive, Dad. Is something bothering you? You aren't ill are you?"

"No, Son, I'm not ill." *Oh what the hell, may as well tell him. I don't want him worrying about my health. Better he know I have a problem of the heart rather than a heart problem.* "I've been worrying about my friend, Helen Whittaker."

"I haven't heard you mention her lately. I wasn't sure if you were still seeing her."

"I'm not, or at least I haven't been lately. When we get back I hope that will change."

"Why did you stop?"

"I wasn't the one who put a stop to it. She did and I don't like it one single bit. I hope to change that situation very soon."

"Is she seeing someone else?"

"I could deal with another man, but it's nothing like that." He went on to explain the situation holding back only the financial part which he felt might embarrass Helen. "I think she's getting carried away with her own success and I'm going to try to make her see that."

"Is she so money-hungry that she can't stop and enjoy life, Dad?"

"No, she's not money-hungry. At least not in the context you're assuming. She's known financial uncertainty in her past and doesn't want to be in that position again. I want her to slow down before her health becomes an issue. In short, I hope to make her realize that I have enough to keep us comfortable for the rest of our lives."

"Are you planning on marrying her, Dad?"

"If she'll have me. If not, then I want us to at least share a common roof so I can take care of her. Our lives are too short to spend apart. I want her to share mine twenty-four hours a day."

"It sounds as if I should meet her. I didn't realize you were thinking this seriously. I thought you were only seeing each other for the odd dinner and evening out. I'm surprised you got this involved without me knowing."

"I'm sorry, Guy. I should have talked to you about her before but I guess I didn't realize how much I actually love her until I was no longer a part of her life."

"Do you think she'll give up her career for you?"

"I won't ask that of her to. All I want is for her to slow down a little, take some time for herself ... and for me."

"Well, good luck, Dad. I hope it works out. Maybe the three of us could have lunch together soon."

"I'd like that, Son."

They were skirting the outer perimeter of Montreal and soon were heading west on Highway 417 toward Ottawa. They decided to take a break for Guy to have some coffee. "I just want to give my eyes a break and my fingers are a little stiff from holding the wheel so tightly."

"There's no need to rush. It looks like the plows have been out and the highway seems to be in pretty good shape. Do you want me to drive for awhile?"

"I'm okay. I'll stretch my legs a little and after a bite to eat and some caffeine, I'll be as good as new."

They did take their time. All things considered there was a considerable amount of traffic on the road. With the holidays over, it would appear that everyone was on their way home. Once on the highway again, Guy turned on the radio to hear the weather situation closer to home. Apparently, to the southwest of Ottawa the precipitation was in the form of freezing rain and some of the lesser roads had been closed to traffic. On the 417, the salt trucks and ploughs were working hard to keep the holiday traffic moving.

Gerald knew Helen had gone to Kingston for the holidays and he believed she was coming back by train sometime today. He decided he would pay her a visit this evening.

They found themselves caught behind a plow which was also throwing salt. It slowed them right down but they decided it was safer than being on the snowy road in front of it. Guy looked at his watch and commented that it would be supper time before they arrived in Ottawa. The closer they got to the nation's capital, the heavier the traffic became. Guy had to turn the defroster up to keep the windshield from freezing. It was a good thing the salt trucks were out in full force as the driving was getting increasingly hazardous.

The programming on the radio was interrupted to broadcast a news bulletin about the Via Rail passenger train being derailed south of Smiths Falls. The damage and possible passenger injuries could not be reported yet as crews had just been dispatched to the scene of the accident.

Gerald paled and put his hand on Guy's arm. "I'm quite certain Helen is on that train."

"Oh, Dad, is there anyone you can call to find out for sure?"

"I'll call one of Helen's friends. If they don't know, maybe one of them will have her daughter's phone number."

"We should be home within a half hour as long as there are no traffic delays."

True to his word, he pulled in front of his dad's building thirty-five minutes later. He parked in the visitor area and helped his dad carry his skis and luggage up to his condo. "Do you want me to stay with you, Dad?"

"No, Guy. I'll feel better when I know you're safely home out of this weather. I'll call you later if and when I find out anything. As soon I get out of these clothes, I'll start making some phone calls."

Guy gave his dad a hug and left. Gerald immediately went to the television and turned to the news channel to see if he could learn anything new. All he could see was the information he already knew trailing across the bottom of the screen.

He was not having much more luck with his phone calls. There was no answer at Olivia's and he was having trouble remembering Margaret's and Sarah's last names. Finally he went out to the lobby to find their names on the board and then he looked them up in the phone book.

There was no answer at Sarah's but he lucked out at Margaret's.

"Margaret, this is Gerald Mercier calling … I'm just fine, thank you. I hope you had a nice Christmas too. The reason I'm calling is to find out if you know when Helen is due back from her daughter's."

"I believe she's supposed to be back some time today, Gerald."

"Do you happen to have her daughter's phone number? I'd like to verify that if I may."

"Are you and Helen on speaking terms again, then? I'm not sure she would want me giving you Ellie's number."

"It's kind of an emergency, Margaret. I really would like to reach her if I can. I will take responsibility if Helen is upset with you but I doubt that will happen."

"Well, I suppose it will be all right. Just a minute while I look it up." He could hear her talking to Sarah in the background.

It took a few minutes to get the number and complete the conversation without tipping Margaret to the possibility of Helen being involved in the train accident. He didn't want to upset the women unnecessarily if she had not in fact taken that train. He wasn't sure the number or times of daily trains running between Kingston and Ottawa.

With shaking fingers, he dialled Ellie's telephone number. A child answered the phone.

"May I speak with your mother, please?"

"Who is this?"

"My name is Gerald. I'm a friend of your grandmother's."

"I have two grandmothers. One was visiting us for Christmas but she left today on the train. We waved at it when she left the train station."

"That's what I was wondering, sweetie. May I talk to your mother now please?"

"Mummy, there's a man on the phone who wants to talk to you. He says Grandma is his friend." A clatter echoed in Gerald's ear as the little girl obviously dropped the phone.

He could hear a woman admonish the child about being careless with the way she put the phone down.

"Hello?"

"Hello, Ellie. This is Gerald Mercier, I'm a friend of your mother's."

"Gerald Mercier? I've heard my mother speak of you. If you're looking for her, she's already left for home. In fact she should be arriving soon."

"Ellie, did she take the train?"

"Yes, it left this afternoon."

"That's what I was afraid of." He sat when his legs threatened to give out from under him.

"What are you afraid of?"

He was trying to think of the best way to word his answer without panicking Ellie.

"Mr. Mercier? What are you afraid of?"

"Ellie, I heard on the radio there has been an accident. I don't know the details but it involves a Via Rail train south of Smiths Falls. I was hoping to find out if it's the one your mother is on."

"What? An accident? Just a minute please."

He could hear her ask someone to turn the television on to the CTV network news channel. As he turned to his own television he could see a helicopter view of a train wreck beneath. He used the remote to turn the sound up.

"Mr. Mercier, can you give me your phone number? I will call you back."

He gave her the number and sat in front of the television in an attempt to learn any details of the accident. Apparently, the most obvious cause for the accident was that a switch had been frozen from the ice and had not locked properly causing the train to derail. Several cars had overturned and the rescue crew was just arriving on the scene to assess the damage and try to rescue the injured passengers. The railway had yet to confirm this was in fact the cause.

Ellie called him back within the hour with confirmation that the train in question was her mother's. She had left her name as a contact for any information about her mother. She assured Gerald that as soon as she heard anything at all, she would call him. They were asking people to stay away from the crash scene to facilitate the arrival and movement of emergency vehicles. As passengers were identified, their families would be notified.

Gerald called Guy to bring him up to date on the situation but refused his offer to keep him company. "I'll feel better knowing you're off the roads. I understand the weather is getting worse and the icy conditions could hamper the rescue efforts. I'll be okay. I think I should let Helen's friends know about this. If they see it on the television they'll worry anyway."

Once again he dialled Margaret's number. "Margaret, it's Gerald again. I wonder if you and Sarah could come to my condo. I need to speak to both of you for a minute." He needed to stay put because he'd given Ellie his home number rather than his cell.

"Is Helen there?"

"No, she's not but that's what I want to talk to you about. Can you spare me just fifteen minutes or so? I'd appreciate it."

"Okay, we'll be right up."

Five minutes later, there was a knock on his door. He let the two ladies in and noted the questioning looks directed at him. They both sat on the sofa and waited for him to speak.

"You both are aware that Helen is on her way home today by train. I'm not sure if you're aware there has been a train accident near Smiths Falls."

"What? Is our Helen on that train? Is she hurt?" Sarah stood up and grasped the sleeve of Gerald's sweater.

"Yes, she's on that train, but I don't know yet if she's hurt."

# Chapter Sixteen

"How can we find out? Oh, dear, poor Helen." Margaret was on the verge of hysteria.

Gerald tried to reassure them even though his own emotions were in a turmoil. "Her daughter has left her name as next of kin with the railway company. She's phoning her brother to let him know before he sees it on the news. VIA Rail assured her they would notify families as quickly as they could identify passengers."

Sarah looked from Gerald to Margaret. "All we can do is wait."

"I just got home from my vacation with my son so I've hardly had time to think about anything but Helen's safety. Can I offer you ladies a drink or a cup of tea?"

Margaret volunteered to make the tea while Gerald unpacked and put away his skis. They all sat in front of the television and watched the news unfolding. The freezing rain let up as the evening progressed but the temperatures had dropped and getting rescue vehicles and personnel to the scene was extremely difficult. It appeared that two passenger cars had remained upright but even the passengers inside those had been tossed about rather badly.

Sarah retrieved a lasagne from her apartment and it was baking in Gerald's oven when the phone rang. Ellie sounded very agitated.

"Someone from the railway called me, Gerald, and my mother was not among the passengers in the upright cars. They were able to identify those people rather quickly. Because of the damage to the part of the train that was derailed and upended, it's going to take awhile for them to get to the others. I'll pass along more information when I receive it, but I don't want to tie up the line in case they try to reach me."

"I understand, Ellie. Margaret and Sarah are here with me and we're watching the television. My first thought was to drive to the scene and offer my help but they're telling everyone to stay away. It's difficult sitting here knowing Helen is only forty-five minutes away. I feel so useless. We'll wait for your next call and don't hesitate, no matter what time it is."

Gerald relayed the information to the women, then sat with his elbows on his knees and rubbed his face and eyes with his hands. He was having a hard time keeping it together in front of Helen's friends. All he could picture was his precious love laying injured in the freezing cold. Why had he not tried harder to make amends with her before they had gone on their vacations? She thought he was intimately involved with Stella Jacobson when all he wanted was the brown-eyed, brown-haired woman who had stolen his heart as a child. Who owned it still.

He looked up to see Sarah watching him.

"You really love her, don't you, Gerald?"

All he could reply was a shaky "Yes."

"She loves you too, you know. Every time I think about how things have turned out for you two, I could just cry."

"I had made up my mind while I was away to ask her to marry me — to insist on it actually. That's all I could think about on the ride home. We've wasted enough time living apart, hardly seeing each other. We're not young and I don't want to spend another day without her."

Margaret had been quietly watching and listening. When she

finally attempted to speak, her voice was shaky and her eyes filled with tears. "I feel responsible for the misunderstanding." She stood in front of Gerald, then placed a hand on his. "I saw you leave Stella's apartment early that morning and was compelled to share that tidbit with Sarah and Olivia. We had you condemned without even giving you a chance to defend yourself. All we were concerned about was protecting Helen from another broken heart. We didn't know whether to tell her about you and Stella or let her find out herself. We thought it might be easier coming from us.

"Oh, Gerald, I am so sorry. The morning that you told her you were coming to her apartment because you had something to talk to her about, Olivia happened to call just after you. To make a long story short, she told Helen about me seeing you leaving Stella's apartment with a bag in your hand at a very early hour. Helen assumed you were coming to tell her about your new relationship and to end things with her. She couldn't bear to hear it. Wanting time to digest what Olivia had just told her and to just plain compose herself, she stayed away all day. She's not been the same since."

"So you all had me tried, found guilty, and sentenced without even knowing the facts."

"I'm afraid so."

The silence hung heavily in the room. Margaret lifted an eyebrow when Sarah glanced warily at her. They waited apprehensively to see if Gerald was going to ask them to leave. If he was not guilty of sleeping with Stella, why would he just not say so? The woman whose cat Margaret had been checking on had confided that she had seen Gerald with his arm around Stella, entering her apartment one other evening. "Right cozy those two have been," was her comment.

"Gerald, do you want us to leave? I wouldn't blame you." Sarah looked askance, hoping he didn't, on both counts.

"No. The only result usually gained by anger is regret. I have to confess, I'm not totally pleased with the chain of events you ladies have unwittingly set off, but we have a common bond in Helen and I know you are as concerned for her well-being as I am. I think there's some comfort in staying together until we hear from Ellie." He stood and smiled. "Besides I wouldn't want to be placed in the position of arm wrestling you for that delicious smelling lasagne."

Both women smiled in return and all three automatically joined arms in a group hug.

# Chapter Seventeen

Helen regained consciousness slowly. The sounds of moaning and crying all around her and the pain she was suffering surely meant only one thing. *That was the sounds of the souls of the dead suffering in hell. I'm dead. I have truly died and ended up in hell.* As she slowly drifted into oblivion again the thought running through her head was, *What was the point in being good all my life when I ended up down here anyway? Maybe this really* is *all there is. Boy, is Margaret gonna be pissed when she finds out.*

However, as her senses returned a little she realized it was too cold to be hell. Ice crystals had formed on her eyelashes and her upper lip felt frozen. As long as she lay perfectly still, her pain was tolerable. Unable to move her legs, she didn't have much choice. Her fingers must be frozen because she couldn't wiggle them. She was twisted with one hip on the floor or ground and one leg on top of the other. Her shoulders were both touching whatever was beneath her. If she really concentrated and put all her effort into it, she could move one shoulder slightly and then the other. That must be a good sign. *If I'm paralysed then maybe it's only from the waist down.*

Was help coming? The realization that the train had crashed or derailed, or both, dawned on her when she lifted her head slightly and could make out some of the dark shapes around her. The last stop she recalled had been Brockville. There was damp cold coming from somewhere above her. It was dark and everything was in shadows, but it appeared the car must have rolled on its side. She tried calling out but her voice just joined the choir of other voices screaming and crying around her. She could hear a baby crying.

Her view was impaired by the seats on either side of her. She remembered being lifted from her seat and almost thrown over the one in front of her before being thrown sideways. She could hear something gritty beneath her head and shoulders. Broken glass? That had to be it. She must be lying with her back against a shattered window. Why couldn't she move her legs?

It was hard to determine how much time had passed. It was impossible for her to stay awake. After drifting in and out of consciousness several times it seemed like it must be hours later. A strong, healthy voice was calling through an open space above her somewhere. Helen tried answering, "Here. I'm here. Help me, please, help me." Other voices cried out around her. She could no longer hear the baby.

She tried to pull herself up but only succeeded in passing out from the pain in her head. By the time she woke again, the noise around her was almost unbearable. The sound of metal on metal reverberated inside her head. She was sure she could smell tar or oil burning. "Stop. Oh, stop, please!" The noise. "Please, somebody, stop the noise." She cried but no one paid her any heed. Maybe she was dead and nobody could hear her.

The wailing and crying she had heard earlier had mostly subsided. Had everyone been rescued or had they … she didn't even want to think of the alternative. Suddenly something shifted near her and pain shot through her body. "Stop, stop!" She cried as loud as she could. "Help me! Oh, God, please help me."

Someone was holding her hand. "They've come to rescue us, Miss. They're having trouble getting inside." A young man was whispering very close to her ear.

The metallic sounds stopped. There were voices once again.

"Can you hear us in there?"

"Yes," she whispered, then louder, "Yes, please help me. I can't move."

A flashlight beam scanned the inside of the car. All Helen could see was crumpled metal and above her several broken windows. "Help, please." She burst into tears.

"Hold on. Don't panic, folks. We're trying to get some equipment in place. We'll have you out of here in no time. I just have to move away for a few minutes. I'm coming right back."

"Don't go. Don't …" The light disappeared and everything was in darkness once again. She could feel someone holding her hand.

She passed out again and vaguely recalled a thump on the ground or floor next to her. Sounds and movement seemed to come and go. Whoever had held her hand was no longer beside her. It seemed like there were fewer voices and cries each time she woke up. The pain in her head and neck was excruciating. A light was once again trained on her and a kindly, male voice cautioned her not to move. Then another thump and a second voice joined the first. She tried to focus but all she could see was two shapes bending over her. They had suns where their heads should be. That can't be right. Helen heard one of the sun men calling out for other survivors. She heard a couple of moans. When she was able to focus a little she realized the sun heads were really lanterns attached to their helmets.

It became a haze of voices, metal sounds and movement all around her. *Gerald. I need Gerald. Where are you? I need you to hug me and tell me everything is going to be all right.* At one point she noticed an intravenous bottle above her and realized someone had tucked a blanket over her. *Thank you, Gerald. Give me your hand again.* She seemed incapable of staying awake for more than a few minutes at a time. Finally, a voice whispered in her ear, "We're going to move you now, Ma'am. Don't be frightened, we've got you strapped in well but we have to lift you up out of the car."

It felt like she was floating on air and then dropped in the middle of a party. So much noise, so many voices barking commands. Sirens. Beepers. Then she was lifted inside a vehicle and someone was sitting beside her. *Gerald?* So much noise.

"Ma'am, can you hear me?"

"Yes." A whisper was all she could produce.

"Can you tell me your name?"

It took a minute for her to think. "Helen. My name's Helen."

"That's good, Ma'am. Do you have a last name?"

Again she hesitated. "Mc … Mc … Allister. McAllister."

"Helen McAllister?"

"Yes." She frowned. Something didn't seem right.

There was more activity around her and more voices. Then movement. She seemed to be at an angle. The noise was very loud. Why couldn't they turn the sound down? Her head hurt.

"Where are we?" She asked the man adjusting her intravenous tubes.

"We're in a helicopter on our way to Ottawa General Hospital, Ms. McAllister. Is there someone we can notify for you?"

"El … my daughter. My daughter's name is El … Elinor." Then she once again lost the battle to keep her eyes open.

"Okay, Dan, we can let them know we're coming in with two more. One, a male, appears to be about mid-thirties with undetermined injuries, vitals are good but appears to be comatose. The other is a woman, probably mid-fifties, name of Helen McAllister, BP's low but stable, injuries to both legs, probable concussion, fading in and out of consciousness. Next of kin is a daughter, name of Elinor. She faded before she could give us a last name. Assume it's the same as the mother. She also mentioned someone named Gerald."

"We'll add her to the rescued and injured list. What's your

ETA?"

"We're about twenty minutes out."

The nurse on duty at the hospital checked on her regularly and insisted on waking her and asking the same questions over and over. All Helen wanted to do was sleep but they kept shaking her awake. One of their concerns was that they were unable to find a record of her on the passenger list nor any record of her daughter Elinor, or Gerald, on the contact list.

# Chapter Eighteen

When midnight came and went and still no word on Helen, Gerald called Ellie to say he was driving to the site to see what was taking so long to get the remaining passengers out. He could sit still no longer. The two women had gone back to Margaret's apartment to keep their own vigil. There was live coverage from the scene and all passengers had long since been dispatched to various hospitals in Ottawa. Ellie had called every one of them without success. Helen seemed to have disappeared from the radar.

Gerald was not about to give up hope. Until they found her body, he was going on the assumption she was still alive. Perhaps she had been thrown a distance from the wreckage. Maybe they weren't searching beyond a small corridor along the track. She could be lying mere feet from where they were looking.

The highway was in excellent shape. The road crews had been working on it to keep it open for all the emergency vehicles. He had to admit, the emergency response workers had reached the sight and rescued all those passengers in record time. They probably had saved many lives with their quick action. He understood the derailment had occurred within two hundred yards of the highway. With luck, they would have some answers for him when he arrived.

About a half mile from the scene, he heard a melody emanate from the dash. Even though he had given Ellie his cell phone number, he was surprised that it was working in this area. Almost afraid to answer, but deciding there was a fifty/fifty chance it could be good news he pressed the speaker button as he slowed to the side of the road.

Ellie was talking almost too fast to understand. "Ellie, slow down, dear. I'm having a hard time making out what you're saying."

"Gerald, where are you? You have to go back."

"What? Why? I'm almost at the sight."

"They found her. She's in the hospital in Ottawa. She's been there for quite a few hours."

"Why did no one call you?"

"She must be confused because she gave them her maiden name and only my first name. My given name, Elinor. They've been trying to identify Helen McAllister on the passenger list and her next of kin, Elinor McAllister. She must have given them your name at some point because they have Gerald on their next of kin list."

In spite of the situation he couldn't help a smile. "You say she's confused? Does she have head injuries?"

"She has a concussion. They won't tell me too much other than her injuries are not life threatening. Gerald, can you go to the Ottawa General? I lied and told them you were her fiancé and that they were to treat you as next of kin."

Gerald blessed the girl for her ability to use her head under trying circumstances.

"I'll turn around and go straight there. I should be there within the hour."

"How's the driving?"

"Not bad at all. I think the road crews have been working to keep them safe for the emergency vehicles. I'll call you after I've seen her and have some answers." He almost hung up but hesitated only a moment before continuing, "Ellie, our prayers have been answered. God will keep us all safe now until we can be together."

"I'll come in the morning. Nick has been standing by but I'll tell him to wait a couple of days before coming, at least until we know how strong she is. If she's not in any danger it's a long way for him to come. Call me as soon as you can, Gerald, please."

"I will, Ellie."

He broke the connection and pulled a U-turn. Suddenly, life seemed much sunnier. Before he was up to speed, he called Margaret's number and gave her the news, promising to call again in the morning after he knew the situation.

Finding a parking spot was almost impossible. Part of the hospital was under renovations so portions of the parking lot were cordoned off. It appeared that half the population of Ottawa was trying to park their vehicles. Finally, he spotted a pickup truck backing out of a spot and almost had a fender bender with a shiny, black Nissan vying for the same vacancy. His bigger car was perhaps a little intimidating because the other driver found his brakes just in time to avoid the collision.

Gerald went through the emergency admitting, giving his name and Helen's. He remembered to give both her married name and her maiden name. Soon he was in the elevator trying not to picture what Helen might look like. He wanted her injuries to be minimal. He wanted her to look her beautiful self. Most of all, he want her to be happy to see him.

When he arrived at her room, he hesitated outside her door and prepared himself for the absolute worst. He wouldn't want to alarm her by cringing at the sight of her. He took a deep breath and walked into her room. His breath caught. She appeared to be sleeping so it gave him time to gaze at her unseen.

There were dark circles around her swollen eyes. Her mouth was puffy and her arms were covered in bandages. One leg lay exposed on top of the blanket and was encased in a splint type apparatus. Bandages covered what must be multiple injuries above and below the splint. She never looked more beautiful to him. Just to know that she was safe and being taken care of blinded him to all the bruises and contusions.

He moved to her side and leaned to kiss her forehead while he reached for her hand. Her eyes opened as far as they could with absolute surprise registered in them. Just as he was about to speak a nurse walked in the door.

"Are you Gerald Mercier?"

"Yes, I am."

"Mrs. Whittaker's daughter called to say her fiancé was on his way. I guess she gave you all quite a scare."

Gerald felt Helen stiffen.

"That's putting it mildly. At least we know she's safe and in good hands now."

"I'll be back to check on her shortly. She has a concussion so we can't let her sleep too deeply. It's easy to slip into a coma." She patted Helen's covered foot and winked. "I guess I shouldn't worry now that Mr. Mercier is here. You probably won't be taking your eyes off him for too long."

When the door closed behind the nurse, Helen raised an eyebrow at Gerald.

"Fiancé?"

"That was Ellie's doing, although I give her full credit for thinking quickly." He noted happily that she had not removed her hand from his.

When Helen just continued to stare at him, he continued, "You must have been confused from your concussion, love. You had given the rescuers your maiden name for identification and you called Ellie, 'Elinor'. I understand you passed out before they could clarify her last name. I understand my name came up in passing as well. You had been listed among the missing, Helen. We were all distraught with worry. I was almost at the accident sight when Ellie reached me on my cell phone to tell me you were here. Somehow she broke through the confusion and gave them your proper identity. Because visitors are very limited and she can't get here till tomorrow, well later today now, she told them I was your fiancé and to treat me like next of kin." He smiled and lifted her hand to his cheek. "I have no objection to that of course."

Her face looked troubled. She attempted unsuccessfully to pull her hand free. After a momentary tug-of-war, she gave up. "Why would she presume to call you my fiancé and why were you and Ellie in conversation in the first place?"

"We both love you, Helen. When I heard about the train wreck on the news, I was frightened because I heard you had gone to Kingston by train and were expected back yesterday afternoon."

"Who told you that?"

"It doesn't matter. I don't really remember anyway." He lied. He was not about to tell her that Stella had filled him in.

"Stella Jacobson."

"I can't remember."

She gave him a knowing look and made another attempt to free her hand. That only prompted him to wrap his other hand around it as well and bring it to his lips.

"How are you feeling, Helen? Are you in much pain?"

"Since I have a concussion they won't sedate me. They're giving me Tylenol for the headache. It helps a little. I'll probably feel worse in another day or two when all the pulled muscles make their presence known."

Gerald's eyes appeared black and opaque through the tears that welled in his eyes. He was squeezing her hand but she didn't complain. If she had been confused before, she certainly was now. Why was he here? Why had he contacted Ellie? Or had she contacted him? Maybe he knew nothing about her accident until

Ellie unwittingly called him. Perhaps he had been put on the spot by her daughter. She had not told Ellie that Gerald had another woman in his life now. Poor Gerald, what an awkward situation in which to be placed. On second thought, to hell with poor Gerald, the man was a first class jerk. She was glad Ellie had trapped him into coming here and pretending to be her fiancé. She would make him squirm. Her eyes were heavy again and she was having trouble keeping them open.

"Did you have a nice holiday with your family, Helen?"

"Hmm?"

"Open your eyes, love. Talk to me."

She opened one eye and smiled wearily. "I had a wonderful time. It was so good, I'm thinking of accepting Ellie's invitation to move there."

He straightened in his chair. "Move to Kingston? What about your business?"

"I think if I move near them, my expenses will be less and I won't need as much income." She closed both eyes again.

"Helen? Helen?"

When no answer was forthcoming Gerald was about to call the nurse when the door opened. The same nurse entered followed by a young doctor. Gerald learned he was the resident who had been assigned to Helen's care, Dr. Glen Dingwall. The young man checked the chart on the table near the door, then lifted her eyelids one at a time and peered inside with a little penlight. After taking a pulse reading, he motioned to Gerald to come back by the bed.

"She appears to be just sleeping at the moment. We can let her rest for half an hour. Will you be remaining here for a while, Mr. Mercier?"

"I will stay as long as I'm allowed. Her daughter is hoping to arrive from Kingston later this morning so I would like to stay until then if I may."

"By all means. Try to keep her talking when she wakes up and please don't let her sleep for longer than thirty minutes at a time. The nurse will be checking her regularly too." The doctor looked again at Helen and commented that she was a lucky woman to escape with only one broken bone and a concussion.

Helen had indeed been among the lucky ones. There were no known deaths, which was phenomenal for the chaotic destruction visible on the television. Three people were still unaccounted for and one hundred and seven had walked away uninjured. Some of the survivors were clinging to life by the merest thread, some had injuries from which they would survive but their lives would change, and others, like Helen, would mend in time and have only memories as souvenirs of the train wreck.

After X-rays and CT Scans, her injuries included one broken leg, deep lacerations to both legs and her arms, a concussion and pulled muscles in her back and neck. She had been thrown from her seat when their car went over on its side and some of the luggage in a storage bin, wrenched loose in the collision, had landed on her legs.

Gerald took advantage of Helen's brief sleep time to go to the cafeteria and get a cup of coffee. It was a long way till morning and he was determined to stay with Helen for as long as he could. While he was out, he remembered his promise to call Ellie and Margaret and found a pay phone to complete the calls.

By the time he returned to Helen's room, twenty minutes had passed so he spent the next ten minutes drinking in the beauty of his long-time love, and willing her mind to forgive him his imaginary transgressions. He was not going to give up without a fight. One way or another, she was going to become a permanent part of his life. As if she had an internal alarm clock, her eyes opened just as he was about to play Prince Charming and kiss her to awaken her.

"Hello, sleepy head." He leaned over and kissed her on the

lips anyway. Startled, she watched as he smoothed a lock of hair from her face.

The nurse came in on schedule and went through her routine procedures. Helen fell back to sleep and this agenda continued through the next several hours. Helen would ask a simple question once in a while such as the time, or to tell Gerald he should go home to bed. At shortly after nine in the morning a striking brunette, who looked vaguely familiar, entered the room and introduced herself as Helen's daughter. Gerald remembered then that he had seen her in pictures at her mother's apartment.

He updated her on Helen's condition as best he could. After her refusal to have him buy her breakfast, he understood that she just wanted the comfort of sitting with her mother. It had been hard on Ellie stuck at home during the rescue procedure. Her husband had arranged for several days off so she could drive up. She had come straight to the hospital and would take her things to her mother's condo later. Gerald decided to leave the women alone and try to catch up on some much needed sleep.

Thinking his parking ticket would require a bank loan to pay, he was pleasantly surprised to learn there was a maximum charge for any twenty-four hour period. He didn't realize just how tired he was until he sat on his bed and removed his shoes. When he unbuttoned his shirt, he realized he still had on the same clothes in which he had dressed the previous morning. Had it really been twenty-four hours? His message light was blinking on his phone which he almost ignored but decided to pick it up in case Ellie had forgotten something. There were two calls from Helen's friends asking for an update on her condition and one from Guy. With a guilty conscience for having neglected to keep Guy in the loop he dialled his son's number.

Phone calls returned, shower taken, an hour later Gerald finally slid between his sheets and instantly fell asleep. When, the sound of the door bell ringing woke him from a deep slumber, a glance at his bedside clock told him he had rested a straight six hours. After slipping into a pair of track pants from the hook behind his bedroom door, he called to his visitor to be patient. He was sorry he had called out, however, when he glanced through the peep hole and saw that the person who had been leaning on his doorbell was Stella Jacobson. Too late to pretend he wasn't home, he forced a smile and opened the door.

"Gerald, have you heard about the train wreck? I just learned that Helen Whittaker was on that train and she's in the hospital." Without invitation, she waltzed by him not stopping until she was in his living room. "Why are you in your track pants? Were you exercising?"

"No, Stella, I was sound asleep." He didn't mean to sound abrupt, but the one thing he didn't want or need right now was the company of this particular person. He may be slow at times, but he wasn't stupid. He knew that if he was to win Helen's heart back, he would have to distance himself from Stella Jacobson.

Clearly startled, Stella frowned. "Well, someone certainly woke up grumpy. I'm sorry, Gerald, but I never would have thought you would be sleeping at five o'clock in the afternoon. I know you and Helen were friends and figured you would want to know about her misfortune."

"I'm sorry too, Stella. I guess I did wake up grumpy but with good reason. I got no sleep last night because I was at the hospital with Helen. I only got home at ten this morning, when I finally fell into bed after almost thirty hours without sleep."

"You were with Helen? How did you know where she was? Did she call you?"

"No. I was beside myself with worry when I learned of the train derailment. I figured she was on her way home at that time. After several conversations with her daughter and a drive to the crash sight, we learned she had been air-lifted to Ottawa General. I did bedside vigil until Ellie arrived this morning."

"Really, Gerald, wasn't that expecting a bit much of you? I know you and Helen had been friends but to have to spend a whole night sitting in a hospital, well, I think her daughter was more than a little presumptuous. You are not a young man after all."

"I did it because I wanted to, Stella. Helen is not just an old friend. She is the woman I intend to make my wife. I love her. I always have." There he had said it. It was out in the open.

Stella gasped and moved her hand to her heart. "You can't mean that, Gerald. You've been spending so much time with me, caring for me. I thought we … I thought … I assumed that you and I meant something to each other. I don't understand."

Gerald felt like a jerk. Worse. An asshole jerk. He hadn't intended to hurt Stella. His patience was just running a little thin and his nerves were on edge.

"Stella, sit down and let me explain." He tried to soften his earlier words by explaining how he and Helen had grown apart for a short time. It had never been his intention to lead Stella on, because as he had said, he was in love with Helen.

"But you let me confide in you. I told you more than I've ever told any other person about myself. You helped me, Gerald. I assumed that was because you cared for me."

"Stella, I do care about you but I'm not in love with you. I tried to help you because I hated to see you heading down a path of no return, or at least a difficult return. As it is, my departure from your apartment very early one morning was seen and misconstrued."

"Gerald, I've been such a fool. I'm so embarrassed and ashamed."

"Please, dear, there is no need to be. I was happy to help you. I will continue to if you need me. I've kept your confidences. No one knows but you and me."

The tears were visible in her eyes. She stood and started

towards the door. With her back to him she murmured, "I was falling in love with you, Gerald. I'm so sorry. I like Helen, envy her in fact. She seems to know what she wants and goes after it. I … I'll keep my distance. You don't have to worry about me embarrassing you."

He walked with her to the door. "I'm sorry too, Stella. You are a fine woman."

She opened the door and started out, then turned back into his arms. With a firm hug, she wished him happiness and kissed him on the mouth. He caressed her cheek and lifted her chin to kiss her gently. "Thank you." He smiled and watched as she walked straight toward Margaret and Sarah who had been watching open-mouthed from the moment Stella had opened his door.

Suddenly feeling very naked in his track pants, bare chest and bare feet, he realized his hair was not combed and that he looked like someone who had in fact, just gotten out of bed.

# Chapter Nineteen

The two women watched as Stella walked by them to the elevator. She barely gave them a nod before lifting her chin high and stepping gracefully between the open doors. Margaret grasped Sarah's arm to keep her from storming Gerald's apartment. When the floor indicator for the elevator stopped at Stella's level and remained there, they walked over, punched the down button and waited for it to return. They hurried to Margaret's suite where both agreed that a strong cup of coffee might not be enough.

"What do you think that was all about?"

"Sarah, I'm afraid to even hazard a guess. I will tell you one thing though, it may have been Stella that initiated that little scene but Gerald sure didn't back away from it. In fact, he kissed her in return — affectionately, I might add."

"Damn, just when I was starting to like him again. How could he carry on like that while poor Helen's lying in the hospital? Didn't he just profess his undying love for her less than twenty-four hours ago?"

"I guess we shouldn't jump to conclusions, but he's looking more and more like a slime-ball to me."

"Do you think we should confront him, Margaret?"

"No. He saw us and chose to ignore us. I think that has guilt written all over it. If he had an excuse for what we just witnessed, he would have waved us over."

"I guess it is true then. He must be involved with Stella. When you saw him in the hallway that morning, he must have been returning home after spending the night with her."

"How will we find out about Helen if we don't talk to him?"

"You have a point." She finished her coffee and accepted a refill when Margaret offered. "Why don't we take a drive to the hospital and see if they'll give us any information. Maybe Ellie is there now and she can fill us in."

"Good idea. I'll go to my place for my coat and boots and meet you downstairs. I think we should take a taxi rather than trying to drive with all the road crews still clearing streets."

An hour later, they approached the desk in the wing of the hospital where they had been informed Helen was quartered. The nurse directed them to a waiting room explaining she couldn't give out any information and promised to let Helen's daughter know they were there.

When Ellie peered into the little waiting room and saw her mother's friends, she felt a rush of relief. These dear women loved her mother like a sister. They exchanged hugs and kisses all around and after a few tears were shed they sat and all started talking at once.

"Okay, Ellie, tell Sarah and me just how Helen is doing. We've been worried sick."

"Did Gerald not fill you in on her condition?"

They looked briefly at each other and in unison shook their heads. Sarah responded first. "We've not had a chance to talk with him. We didn't want to bother him after his tiring night."

"Of course, the poor man must be exhausted. He was up all night and stayed with Mom until I arrived late this morning. He wouldn't leave her alone for one minute."

Sarah and Margaret exchanged a brief look but managed to keep their disgust from showing. Before either could speak, the nurse poked her head in the door.

"Ellie, your mother's fiancé is on the phone. Did you want to talk to him?"

"Sure, I'll take it in the hallway." She excused herself saying she'd be right back.

"Fiancé?"

The women stared at each other wondering what in the devil was going on.

"Margaret, we better not say anything until we know more about this."

"You're right. I am so confused. I wish Olivia was here. She has a way of getting to the heart of any situation."

"I think it's time we called her anyway. She will be one angry woman when she gets back and finds we kept this from her."

When Ellie returned, the women turned to her with equally confused expressions.

"Fiancé? Did Helen become engaged while she was away?"

Ellie laughed as she sat across from them. "No, she didn't. Not officially." She glanced from woman to woman and was puzzled by the less than delighted expressions on their faces. "I better explain. I knew I wouldn't be able to get up here right away but Gerald was so frantic to find my mother and learn her condition. I knew the hospital would not tell him anything unless he was next of kin, so I told them Mother's fiancé was on his way and to treat him as family. The poor man didn't seem to mind when I told him. In fact, he seemed quite pleased."

"I see." Margaret tried to smile but her attempt was only half-hearted.

"Gerald will be here in another hour to relieve me so I can freshen up at Mother's apartment and try to get some rest. He'll probably stay with her until she's settled for the night. The doctor feels the immediate concern about her concussion is over and if she shows no worrisome symptoms by midnight, they'll let her sleep without interruption."

"That is good news, Ellie. Have they given you any indication how long she might be hospitalized?"

"No. She may be transferred to a regular room sometime tonight and I understand her leg won't be a real problem. She'll need care at home, but I'm hoping she might be released within a couple of days."

"Will you being staying for awhile?"

"I'll talk to Gerald about Mom's care. I can stay for a few days but I'll have to go home again so Willis can get back to work. I'll arrange for home care for her and I'm hoping Gerald can fill in the blanks. He sounds quite willing to stay with her as much as is needed."

Margaret, holding back her desire to question Gerald's intentions, stood up and offered Ellie a hug. "Please tell Helen we were here and that we're praying for her quick recovery. If there is anything we can do, you know any one of us will be happy to help. If Gerald is unable to stay with her, perhaps Sarah and I can take turns."

"I know I can count on all of you. I hate to impose on your friendship."

Sarah spoke up. "It's no imposition. If anything, it would be a good excuse to play non-stop cards."

"Okay. I'll see what Gerald wants to do."

Ellie managed to get permission for Sarah and Margaret to slip inside Helen's room to see for themselves and be reassured that she really was in satisfactory condition. Each squeezed the toes on her good leg while she slept, then left.

They arrived at their condominium complex just in time to see Gerald crossing the foyer to catch a cab. Unsuccessfully, the women tried avoiding him. He caught Margaret's arm and asked if Helen was awake when they left the hospital. She pulled her arm free and looked at him as if he had the plague. "Go see for yourself, you … you … Casanova."

"Look, ladies, I don't have time for this conversation right now, but what you saw is not what you think it is. Once again, you are judging and condemning without knowing the facts. Will you give me the benefit of the doubt for now and maybe we can discuss this tomorrow?"

"You don't owe us any explanation at all. That poor woman in the hospital is the only one we're concerned about right now. If you hurt her one more time, Gerald Mercier, you may as well move back to Montreal because life will not be pleasant for you around here. In the meantime, keep your hands off me and your explanations to yourself." With that she nudged Sarah toward the elevators.

# Chapter Twenty

Gerald arrived at the hospital just as Helen was waking. Ellie gave her mother a hug along with assurances she would be back first thing in the morning. She motioned Gerald to follow her into the hallway and questioned him about his availability and willingness to spend some time with her mother if she was allowed to go home within the next few days.

"I'll gladly stay with her twenty-four hours a day. You'll just have to hire a professional to do whatever healthcare is necessary. I can cook meals and help her with everything else."

"You wouldn't mind? It's asking a lot from you."

"Ellie, you don't even have to ask. I want to care for your mother. It's something I've been asking her to let me do since we became re-acquainted. I love her and there is nothing I won't do for her."

"Okay. I'll have to run it by her of course, unless you would prefer to discuss it with her. She may listen to you better than me. She's so damn independent all the time."

"I'll test her mood and pick my time."

Ellie laughed and gave his arm a squeeze. "Okay, Gerald, I will leave it with you. Hopefully, she'll listen to reason." She turned to go then faced him again. "The only positive I can see coming out of all of this is that she may be forced to let up a bit with that placement agency of hers and take some time off."

"That's kind of a sore spot with us, so I think I'll leave that one alone for awhile. I will try to make her understand the necessity for around-the-clock care for a couple of weeks."

When he approached Helen's bed, Gerald noticed a slight upturn of lips. "Is that a hint of a smile I see there?"

Helen reached for his hand. When he slid it into hers, she brought it to her cheek and held it there. He couldn't believe the warm welcome he was receiving. Her eyes were locked on his as she whispered, "Will you stay with me when they let me out of here?"

"Helen, do you feel you have to ask? Silly woman, you should know the answer to that."

A tentative smile was edging its way across her bruised face. When she seemed to have trouble making eye contact, he asked, "You're not getting shy with me are you, Helen?"

"No." Her smile deepened and then her eyes locked on his once again. "I've had a lot of time to think while I've been laying here, Gerald."

"What have you been thinking about, love? Not worrying about your homecare I hope."

"We've been drifting apart. I know I've neglected you terribly and that I really have no business asking you to stay with me but …"

"No buts, Helen. I want to stay with you. I always have."

"What about Stella Jacobson?"

Gerald sighed. "It seems Stella has been the centre of a great deal of misunderstanding."

"It's *my* understanding that you and she have been seeing a lot of each other — not that I blame you. I guess I selfishly took for granted that you would always be there." Tears filled her eyes. "When I found out that you and Stella were dating and that you had even spent at least one night with her, well, I needed some time away from here and decided to spend Christmas with Ellie and her family."

She kissed his hand and held it even more tightly. "I love you, Gerald, and I don't want to lose you." She turned away, took a deep breath that held a hint of a sob. "God, I've made a mess of things, haven't I?"

Gerald took a tissue from the bedside table and wiped the tears from her eyes. "We've had a little detour is all." He kissed her forehead. "I love you too, Helen. You already know that. When you're released from this place I'll show you how much I love you."

"Do you know if they'll let me go home soon?"

"Ellie seems to think it might be in a couple of days."

"Good thing my business is shut down till after the holidays."

"Now don't go worrying about your business just yet. Our main concern is getting you back on your feet."

It was nearing midnight when Gerald felt a hand on his shoulder. It was the nurse with news that Helen was sound asleep and probably would not awaken anytime soon. She would be transferred to a regular room before change of shift in the morning. After receiving assurances that the hospital staff would call him if she should need him during the night, he left.

He managed to get inside his apartment without encountering any of the women he had crossed paths with earlier. Wondering how he managed to become involved in such a tangled web of female emotions, he poured himself a stiff drink and turned on the late news.

Margaret and Sarah had called Olivia who was devastated about Helen's accident. The other two assured her there was no reason for her to rush home, that Helen might even be released in a couple of days. Olivia then asked about her home care. Before calling they had agreed to keep the news of Gerald's involvement to a minimum and definitely not to mention the scene with Stella Jacobson. However, with a brief shrug of her shoulders and with a cynical smile on her face, Margaret flatly stated, "Helen's fiancé will be moving in to take care of her twenty-four hours a day."

After a brief pause Olivia responded uncertainly, "Helen's fiancé? Did I hear you right?"

Ignoring Sarah's glare, Margaret continued, "Yes, at least according to Ellie. We haven't got it from the horse's mouth yet. Or maybe I should say horse's ass."

"Okay, come clean. Tell me everything."

It was Sarah, however, who blurted out the story of Gerald's concern and his vigil at the hospital, then about the tender scene with Stella Jacobson in his doorway.

"That two-timing, dirty, rotten … Is Ellie aware that her mother's fiancé has a girlfriend tucked away on another floor of the same building?"

"Of course not. Margaret and I didn't think it was our place to tell her. We really didn't know what to do because we don't want Helen hurt again. We don't think she's well enough to take another blow like that. We did give him a good speaking to though."

"That's it. I'm coming home. Nobody can treat a friend of ours that shabbily and get away with it. I'll see if I can get a flight out of here tomorrow and I'll call you with the flight time and number in the morning. Gerald will never take advantage of another woman by the time we get through with him. He'll be packing his bags and heading back to Montreal. Men. Now you know why I can't be bothered with them."

# Chapter Twenty-one

As it turned out, Olivia's return was delayed by a day. The weather system that had moved through had left disruptions in air travel in its wake and it was impossible to get an immediate flight home. By the time she arrived, Helen had been moved to a regular hospital room and was allowed to sit in a chair for a short while.

The other two women plus Ellie visited as a group and sat for an hour listening to Helen tell about her fun-filled Christmas with her family. Ellie adding items Helen forgot. When they asked her about the train accident, Helen hesitated.

"I don't really remember exactly what happened. I was sitting in my seat one minute and the next I was watching sleet come through a broken window above me. There was noise. People moaning and crying. I thought I was in hell. It didn't dawn on me at first that it doesn't snow in hell. Not the one we've been taught about anyway."

"What's the last thing you remember while you were sitting in your seat?" Ellie was concerned about her mother's seeming loss of memory.

"I remember thinking that I must beg Gerald to forgive me for neglecting him. I could hardly wait to get home to him, hoping desperately it wasn't too late for us to start over."

Before Sarah or Margaret had an opportunity to speak, Ellie patted her mother's arm and said, "I don't think so, Mom. He certainly jumped at the opportunity to help with your home care. That man doesn't appear to consider your relationship over. When he phoned me about the possibility of you being on that train, he was positively devastated. I don't know what's been going on between you, but believe me when I say that man is deeply in love with you."

"Well, he seemed involved with one of our neighbours and I wasn't sure how far that had gone. He says there's been a misunderstanding. I'll have to hear the whole story but for now I'll give him the benefit of the doubt."

The two older women gave each other a look but didn't say anything more. Olivia arrived an hour later and the hugging and stories began once again. The afternoon passed quickly and then a nurse came in accompanied by Gerald. The air in the room became still. Ellie finally, commented that she was tired and looking forward to putting her feet up at her mother's place. She gave her mother and Gerald a hug and left. The three other women agreed it was time to go and bade Helen good-bye without comment or greeting to Gerald.

When they were alone, Helen turned to Gerald and commented on a definite chill in the air upon his arrival. He moved a couple of the chairs away from the bed, pulled his favourite one to her bedside and took his time removing his coat. Then he sat and took her hand.

"Helen, what I'm about to tell you is confidential. It's between you and me and it's never to be discussed with your lady friends. You must promise me this."

"My goodness, Gerald. This sounds rather sinister. What am I promising to keep secret?"

"It's a confidence involving Stella Jacobson."

"Stella? Are you certain I want to hear this?"

"I'm certain you *have* to hear it if we're going to move forward. What I absolutely need to know is that no matter how curious your friends get about my relationship with Stella, it must remain between the two of us."

"Your relationship with Stella? So you are about to tell me one actually exists then."

"Not the kind you're thinking about. At least not on my part."

"It sounds like it might continue?"

"It might."

"Hate to break this up but we have to take Mrs. Whittaker away for awhile." Two nurses, one male, one female came through the door pulling a gurney with them.

"What? Where are you taking me?"

"The doctor wants new X-rays of your limbs and a possible CT Scan of your head."

"Now? Can't it wait till after visiting hours?" She was upset that Gerald was about to spill the beans on Stella and now she was being whisked away.

"The radiology department doesn't hold visiting hours sacred. When there's an opening we are summoned and must run. Sorry."

"But … How long will this take?"

"We never know. It might be all done in an hour or it could take two maybe even three."

"Gerald, you may as well go. I feel badly that you drove all the way here."

"I didn't actually. I took a cab. I found by the time I drive and pay for parking, sometimes at the far end of the lot, it's more convenient to take a taxi. Don't worry, I'll talk to Ellie and maybe I can come early tomorrow and give her a day off. You'll be tired by the time they're through with you and will probably want to sleep anyway."

Looking at her concerned expression, he leaned over and kissed her tenderly. "Don't worry. We'll continue this conversation tomorrow. We *will* be together, Helen, one way or another."

She smiled and kissed his hand before they elbowed him out of the way.

"Sorry to do this Mr. Whittaker, but the doctor needs fresh X-rays so he can work out a therapy program for your wife."

The sound of Helen's soft laughter followed him out of the room.

# Chapter Twenty-two

"What do you think we should do?" Margaret was concerned that Ellie was being caught up in Gerald's charm. "We can't just stand by and say or do nothing."

"I really don't think we can do anything. It's just going to have to work itself out."

"How can you say that, Sarah? Aren't you concerned that Helen is going to be duped by this man? He walked out on her once. His carrying on with Stella Jacobson can't be called innocent when they're kissing each other and he's dressed in hardly more than his underwear. What possible explanation can there be for something like that? He's going to hurt her. Just like he did before and just like Edward did last year. How much more can that poor woman take? She's our friend and we can't let it happen. We just can't."

"And what are we going to tell her, that we saw Stella Jacobson coming out of his apartment, him bare-chested, wearing only track pants and then they kissed each other? How do you think she'll feel? She was just in a train wreck — I don't want her to *become* a train wreck. I think we should give it a couple of days and make sure she's up to it before we tell her."

The phone rang. Olivia let them know she was on her way to join them.

"I need a drink. Sarah, what have you got? Between the crowded airport and the rush to the hospital only to have *him* arrive and cut our visit short, I'm done in."

"As a matter of fact, I've got the fixings for your favourite martini. I may even join you. How about you, Margaret?"

"No, thank you. My stomach hasn't been right lately. I think I might have an ulcer."

"Have you seen the doctor?"

"Yes. He gave me some Tagamet and told me to lay off anything spicy. He's going to run a series of tests. I think all this worry with Helen is just upsetting my system."

Sarah offered her a cup of peppermint tea and mixed Olivia's martini. "Margaret thinks we should tell Helen about Gerald and Stella."

Olivia plucked the olive from her drink. "What do you think, Sarah?"

"I think Helen is suffering enough right now. Why pile more on her plate?"

"He's moving in to take care of her. Maybe he is genuinely in love with her." Olivia kicked off her shoes and set her drink on the coffee table. "Maybe he's caught up in something with Stella from which he's having a hard time breaking free. Maybe we should ask him about it and offer to help — see what he says. Then again, maybe Helen wouldn't like us meddling."

"Too many maybes." Sarah's brow furrowed. "We could always fill Ellie in on what's going on and get her opinion. She wouldn't want her mother hurt by Gerald if it can be avoided."

"You may be right." Margaret added. "I think we should go up and talk to her before this goes any further. After all, Helen may be home in a couple of days."

"I was just about to suggest I pull a quiche out of the freezer. Why don't we invite her down to join us for a bite of supper?"

Two hours later, Sarah had cleared the table and was about to pour coffee all around when Ellie pushed her chair back a bit. "Okay. Let's have it. You all have something on your mind. I felt the freezer click on when Gerald walked into Mom's room this afternoon."

"Ellie, honey, we've been in a quandary over what to do about your mom and him." Olivia put her hand over Ellie's on the table.

"What kind of a quandary? What's going on?"

They took turns telling her what they knew about the relationship between Gerald and Stella Jacobson.

"You think he's having an affair with this Stella person while he's in love in with my mother?"

"We're not sure, Ellie, but it sure appears that way. Especially when the latest episode happened just after he left your mother at the hospital. If Margaret and I hadn't seen it with our own eyes, we might think it was just gossip. There's definitely something going on and we don't want your mother hurt."

"He knows you saw her leaving after kissing her?"

"Yes. He looked right at us, guilty as sin."

"Then I must have a heart to heart with Mr. Gerald Mercier."

❣❣❣

"Hello, Gerald. I hope you weren't sleeping."

"No, I wasn't. Come in, come in." He opened the door and waved Ellie in. "Have you talked to your mother this evening?"

"Yes, just briefly. She was tired from being jostled about for her X-rays and scan. They had given her something for her pain and she sounded half asleep. Hopefully, she'll get a good night's sleep and feel fresher tomorrow."

"Can I get you something to drink? Tea? A glass of wine?"

"No, thank you. I just had coffee at Sarah's. Mom's friends invited me for dinner."

"They are good friends. They and your mom look after each other really well."

"Yes. They're very protective of each other."

"I sense a tone of reproval in that statement."

"Gerald, I'm not going to beat around the bush. I came here to ask if there's any truth to their claim you are having an affair with a woman who lives in the building."

# Chapter Twenty-three

Gerald ran his hand through his hair then motioned for Ellie to take a seat on the sofa. She hesitated briefly but decided she had best hear him out no matter how long it took. She hoped there was a reasonable explanation since she couldn't help liking the man.

"Ellie, your mother is aware that I've had an involvement with Stella Jacobson. She asked me about it again this afternoon and before I could talk to her, I was ushered out so she could be taken for X-rays."

"So it's true then?"

"Yes and no."

"I would think it's either yes or no. Gerald, I don't want you playing cat and mouse with me or my mother. She was hurt terribly by my philandering father and I don't want her suffering that kind of heartache again. You told Mom you love her yet you're seen kissing another woman as she's leaving your apartment just hours later."

"Ellie, give me time to talk to your mother. I owe it to her to discuss this with her first, actually, her only. If she can understand then all I can ask is for you to trust her and me and leave it at that. It's not my confidentiality. It's Stella's. I made a promise I'm not about to break. Believe me when I say I do love your mother. I want to marry her. I want her in my life till death do us part.

Ellie looked at him for the longest time.

"Please?" He held her eyes with his. She liked what she saw. She trusted what she saw.

"Gerald Mercier, if you break my mother's heart, you'll break mine as well. She may forgive you. I never will."

"It won't happen. Trust me. Please."

"I trust you."

He opened his arms and she let him embrace her.

At the door he smiled. "I don't think Helen's friends ever will."

"I'll run interference for you."

Ellie made a detour to Sarah's apartment. Margaret was still there. Olivia, tired from her travels had gone home to bed.

"It's going to be okay. I can't explain. There's a confidence involved. Just trust me. He loves her and it's all going to work out."

Sarah and Margaret looked at each other then nodded.

"Thank you for caring so much about my mother. I appreciate it."

Margaret left to grab the elevator with Ellie after hugs were exchanged.

❣❣❣

Gerald poured a stiff drink for himself and took it into the bedroom. He had just gotten comfortable in bed after finding the news channel when his phone rang.

"I couldn't go to sleep without telling you I love you."

"I thought you would be out for the night."

"Are you in bed?"

"Yes."

"Do you have your pyjamas on?"

"Why, Helen, did you call to have telephone sex?"

After a slight hesitation, "and if I did?"

"Give me a minute to find some music and I'll turn the lamp off."

"Wow." Gerald could hear the rustling of her bedclothes. "I'm almost embarrassed to say I called for something as mundane as to ask if you would mind running up to my condo to pick up a few things to bring with you in the morning. However …"

He stifled a laugh and pretended a groan instead. "I'm afraid the mood has passed."

"Sorry."

"Does Ellie know what you need?"

"I'll call her and ask her to have them ready." Gerald always managed to take her breath away, teasing or not.

❣❣❣

It took most of the morning for Gerald to tell Helen the story of his relationship with Stella Jacobson. Between hospital staff interruptions and Helen's questions he finally got it all out and was waiting for her response. It was a long story about the connection Stella had developed with Gerald through his history of volunteerism with the Mission to Seafarers. Stella had lost contact with a son who had chosen to divest himself of his family and take to a life on the seas. Stella's husband had blamed her and became physically and mentally abusive. When she couldn't take anymore and finally left, the shame and self-blame of having lost the love and respect of the two men she cared about most in life had driven her to drink and eventually to the streets. Because of the influence of a caring chaplain at a Seafarers' Mission in Europe, her son, newly diagnosed with colon cancer, had sought her out after a separation of thirteen years. He took her off the streets. After reuniting they lived happily for almost two years in a small home he bought before he succumbed to his illness. He had never married so when he passed, Stella was the beneficiary of his investments, the home they had lived in, and his insurance policy. Stella was able to sell the small home which she found difficult to stay in after her son was gone. With the proceeds from that and the income from his investments she was able to buy the condo she now occupied. However, the guilt and shame of having been spurned by two men in her life left her with a self-esteem problem. The alcoholism, while under control, was always there. When Stella learned that Gerald had spent his life on the seas and had volunteered at a Mission for Seafarers in Montreal, she immediately felt a bond that had become almost an obsession. Especially so when she learned he had left a family behind when he took to working on the boats. Fighting alcoholism and depression were constants with her even though she managed to hide both quite well. She had mistaken Gerald's friendship and compassion for something deeper. He was finding it difficult to pull back without hurting her. December and Christmas had always been a difficult time for her and this year had been no exception.

"When your friends saw her coming from my apartment, she had just come to tell me about your accident. I told her then how I felt about you and that I hoped to spend the rest of my life with you."

He stood and walked to the window. Helen didn't interrupt his thoughts.

"I felt like a real jerk. She was devastated. However, she did tell me that she likes you and envies your determination to make something of yourself. She went out the door, then turned back and gave me a kiss good-bye. Stella wished us happiness, Helen. That's what Margaret and Sarah saw."

He ran his hand through his hair. "I was startled when I saw them standing there and thought 'Shit, I must look guilty as hell.' So I just turned and went back inside."

Helen sat up and watched him soundlessly for several minutes. When he didn't move, she slid off the bed and hobbled to him. Her arms seemed to wrap themselves around his waste and her lips found his all on their own. She couldn't possibly have loved this man more than at this very moment.

"I am so sorry."

"It's me who should be apologizing."

"I'm not apologizing to you. I'm voicing how sorry I am about my attitude toward Stella for the past year or so that she's lived in our building. We judged her and labelled her without even knowing her. We joked about her and avoided her. How cruel we were!"

This time she reached for her crutches and circled him to stare out the window. When she turned to look at Gerald, there were tears in her eyes.

"You aren't the jerk, Gerald. We are. My friends and I. How cruel we've been. So self-righteous and judgmental. I've been feeling sorry for myself because my husband left me but I had the support of my friends and family to see me through. Poor Stella, she was rejected by her son *and* her husband and had no one to help her. Then to find her son only to lose him again. I can't imagine what she's been through. I am so ashamed."

She leaned on her crutches and put her hands out. "How can I make things right? What can I do?"

"You had no way of knowing, Helen. She doesn't judge you and as far as she's concerned you know nothing about her past. Better just to leave it be. Maybe a smile and a pleasant word now and again will go a long way to making her feel like she's among people who accept her."

He took a tissue from the table and wiped her eyes.

"Now, we have to talk about getting you out of here and home where I can take proper care of you."

# Chapter Twenty-four

Gerald remained with Helen until early afternoon when Ellie arrived. During their respective visit times they took turns helping her walk with her crutches a little farther down the hallway and back each time. By evening she was completely done in but proud of her progress.

Her friends called during the day and she assured them there was no need to make the trek to the hospital because she would probably see them at home the following day. However, that statement proved erroneous as she was not released until another day had passed.

Gerald and Ellie arrived together late in the morning to take her home. Margaret, Olivia and Sarah dropped in with baking, a warm ham and a casserole just before dinner. None even looked at Gerald but chatted non-stop with Ellie and Helen for an hour before leaving.

Ellie told Gerald she would look after her mother that night but he could take over the next day so that she could go home to her children. Helen did not sleep well that night. Her whole body ached and she realized the jarring it had taken when thrown around in the train was finally taking its toll. She didn't argue when her daughter gave her an extra pain killer in the wee hours of the morning which finally allowed her to fall into a deep sleep.

Gerald arrived around 9 o'clock and Ellie left for home an

hour later. She wasn't long gone when the doorbell rang. Gerald opened the door to find Stella Jacobson standing outside with a covered plate in her hand.

"Oh, Gerald, I'm sorry. I thought Helen's daughter was staying with her."

"She just left, Stella. She had to get back to her family and asked if I could help out with Helen in her absence."

"I baked a few things for Helen. Will you give them to her please?"

Gerald hesitated for a moment then from behind him he could hear Helen calling, "Who's at the door, Gerald?

"It's Stella Jacobson. She has some baking for you."

"Oh, please ask her to come in."

Stella appeared uncomfortable but stood her ground. Gerald smiled and motioned her inside.

"Stella, how nice of you to drop by. Your baking is always the best."

"Hello, Helen. I wasn't sure if you were up to company. I tried to catch your daughter but I understand she's already left."

"Yes, she had to get back but I'm glad you didn't just drop the baking and leave." She smiled and pointed to a chair. "Sit down and tell me about your Christmas."

Stella relaxed a little and sat in the indicated chair. Gerald reached for the plate and offered to put the coffee pot on. After making sure, Helen was comfortable and both women had coffee, he left them alone while he went downstairs on the pretence of checking his phone messages.

The women chatted hesitantly at first then found common ground and loosened up. Gerald returned just as Stella was about to enter the elevator.

"Did you have a good visit?" he asked.

"Yes. Helen is very friendly. She asked me to come back later in the week with my recipe for the tarts." Before the elevator door closed she turned and looked at Gerald. "I mean it when I say I hope you and she are happy together. You are both good people."

The doors closed before he could respond. He should have been happy Stella accepted the relationship he and Helen shared but he couldn't help weighing a sense of sorrow against the happiness. Stella had not had an easy life and he had unintentionally added to her distress. She deserved much better and he hoped someday soon she would find it.

The phone was ringing as he let himself into Helen's condo and went in search of her when he heard the answering system click in. The message was from someone wondering when her office would be open again. "Never. If I had my way about it."

"Gerald, that's a conversation I had hoped to put off for a little bit but maybe it's best we deal with it now."

"Conversation? What conversation? You know you are in no shape to go back to work anytime soon, Helen."

She patted the sofa beside her and reached her hand out to guide him to her side. By the contrite look in her face, he was fully expecting a dialogue from her about how she can't neglect her clientele and she must put them before her own discomfort. Of course she would be feeling responsible for all these people who had accepted seasonal employment and who now were out of work. Well, he wasn't going to allow that to happen.

"I know that, Gerald."

She was looking him directly in the eye. "While I was in Kingston with my family, I just couldn't seem to get into the spirit of Christmas. Everyone was enjoying the holiday and the fact we were all together. Ellie went overboard on the food and the children were so excited to have their gramma with them and all I could do was brood." She twisted a tissue in her hands and continued working it in silence for the longest time. "I couldn't figure out why I was in such a funk. I should have been having the time of my life with my family."

The clock in her foyer began to chime out the hour. Noon. Gerald broke the stand-off by looking down at her hands before lifting his gaze to hers again. He wondered if that message on the telephone was going to make or break his day.

"Have you figured it out now?"

"I was missing the man I love. I was not only missing him but frightened to death that I had lost him forever."

"And now?"

"Now I am so utterly angry with myself for letting these past months go by without telling him every single day how I feel."

"And now?"

"Now I am so grateful that he still loves me and wants me that I intend to make it all up to him and to tell him doubly every day how much I love him."

"How about showing him instead of telling him?"

"Gerald Mercier, you are going to be shown so often, you'll grow tired of it and rue the day I gave up my career for you."

"Gave up your career? Do I dare hope this means you are closing your office?"

"Not closing it, Gerald. Selling it. Stella is interested in taking it over."

"What? Stella? I wasn't downstairs for more than an hour."

"I had already made up my mind on the train just before the accident. All it took was for me to find someone to take it off my hands so all my clients aren't left hanging. When Stella offered to help me out till I'm back on my feet again, it didn't take much convincing for her to agree to buy it. Did you know she worked for the government in the unemployment office years ago?"

"So this means we'll be going to Greece in the spring?"

"Greece?"

"Did you not open the gift I left for you before Christmas?"

Gerald watched as she moved her foot then glanced around

the room. "I left it on this table when I went away. I wonder if Ellie put it somewhere."

Gerald went into her bedroom and found it on top of her dresser hidden by the bag of personal items from the hospital. "I'll give it to you again if you promise not to throw it across the room."

She took his hand as he passed the gift to her and kissed his palm. "It sounds like it might be something fragile."

Her hands shook slightly as she untied the ribbon. When she opened the box a smile played across her face. "A teapot, Gerald? Am I supposed to put it high on the shelf and only use it for special company? You perhaps?"

"You're supposed to take the lid off and see what's inside."

When she did, there was a gift card with three words on it written in a neat masculine slant. *Please say yes.* The card was taped to an envelope. When she opened it, there were two airline tickets to Greece.

"Greece?"

"I was hoping we might take a Grecian cruise for our honeymoon."

"Honeymoon?"

"You know, the trip couples usually take right after their wedding?"

"Wedding?"

"That ceremony where two people become one after saying 'I do'."

"Yes."

"Yes?"

"Yes to Greece. Yes to a honeymoon cruise. Yes to saying I do."

"When?"

"As soon as I can walk."

"Should we plan a shipboard wedding?"

"No. I want our family and friends at our wedding but I sure don't want them tagging along on our honeymoon. We can get married at the cathedral as soon as it can be scheduled."

He sat beside her. "I was afraid I'd never hear those words." His cheeks were wet with tears. "I still won't breathe easy until I have a ring on your finger and a marriage certificate in my hand."

"Where will we live?"

"Helen, it doesn't matter to me. We can live here or at my place, or find a completely different place. All that matters to me is that we're together."

"I don't want to leave this building. It's home to me but I don't want to live in this apartment. Maybe your place would be best. I did find your bed comfortable. Very comfortable." She placed her hand under his chin and drew him to her for a kiss.

# Chapter Twenty-five

In the end, the date was set for Valentine's Day. Her children were notified and her condo was placed on the market. Nick agreed to come and give her away and Ellie agreed to be her matron-of-honour. When they saw how happy she was, Helen's friends agreed to give Gerald another chance at making her happy.

Everything started to move forward. Her wounds were healing and she was able to get around on crutches. It was time to tell her friends about her decision to sell her business … and to whom.

After Helen and Gerald both sat with the women and explained that there were extenuating circumstances concerning the relationship between Gerald and Stella Jacobson that would remain confidential, the women grudgingly agreed to give her a chance. Stella took over the operation of the placement agency with Olivia's help, who agreed to stay on until after Easter to assist her until she was able to go forward on her own.

All was good in the world until the day Helen's lawyer called. "Helen, I just received a notice from Irene Urquhart's lawyer. She's filing a motion to include hers and Edward's child as an heir to his estate."

"What? Edward has been dead for over a year and all of a sudden there's a child on the scene?

"Yes. Apparently she gave birth to a baby boy last July."

"Oh my God, Shirley. What in the …? Can she do this?"

"It depends on a number of things, the first of which is proving paternity."

"I don't understand. Why would she wait this long to come forward? There's something fishy about this. Edward didn't leave an estate. She must know this. What does she want?"

"I'm afraid I don't have any answers to your questions. I just received the notice and felt compelled to pass it along in light of your impending marriage, the sale of your condo and any assets you and Gerald may be disposing of or sharing with each other. Ms. Urquhart sure knew when to strike. We have to talk about how to proceed with this."

Helen stood with the phone to her ear and stared out the window. "Shirley, I need time to digest this. Can I call you back?"

"Certainly. I'll be in the office for several more hours. You have my cell phone number if you call after I leave."

"Thank you. It's just … I just can't … I find this so bloody unbelievable. I'll call you later." She hung up.

Gerald came in a short while later and found her sitting on the sofa, head resting in her hands. "Headache?"

"That's an understatement. Headache doesn't begin to describe it."

She explained the phone call in full detail — at least as much as she knew. "I have no idea what's going on. The saying goes that you can't draw water from a stone. Edward left me no money — no estate. What's she after?"

With Gerald's help, she stood and wrapped her arms around his waist. "I thought Edward and Irene were a thing of the past. I had hoped that part of my life was over." She reached for her crutches and moved to the window. "My initial reaction when Shirley told me this was the urge to laugh. I couldn't help but think this was a sick joke of some kind. Irene called me months ago wanting to talk to me about something and I cut her off by telling her to talk to my lawyer. I wonder why she didn't come forward when she first knew she was pregnant."

"Perhaps she had ideas of pulling money out of you then."

"You may be right. Gerald, but I had no money to give her. God knows, I had to go out to work just to support myself."

"She may not have known that. Edward had been supporting her and then died just weeks after moving in with her. She probably assumed he was loaded. The woman was used to Edward paying for everything but once he was gone, she had no legal grounds to go after any of his estate. I doubt they could be considered legal common-law partners and he had not changed his will to include her. This may be a means of getting her hands on anything of his that his children would be entitled to."

"There's just something that doesn't ring true here."

"I assume your lawyer is looking into all of this for you?"

"I told Shirley I'd call her back. I just couldn't think straight when she called. I don't even know what the legal ramifications are. The only asset really that I have is the condo. If she thinks I'm going to turn over any of the proceeds from the sale to her, she's going to have a long wait. She already got everything else we ever owned and all of our savings. Edward spent everything including his RRSPs on her and when that wasn't enough he racked up a huge credit card debt. No wonder he didn't want the bills coming to our home. I'm still paying off the debt for *her* furniture, *her* clothes, *her* jewels, *their* travel and restaurants. And all this time I was sitting at home." She looked at him with fire in her eyes.

"No, damn it! Enough is enough!" She crossed her arms in front of her. "If I have to spend every cent from the sale of this condo on legal fees, I will. I will tie her up in the courts for so long she'll be sorry she ever started down this road. She will not see. One. Red. Cent!"

"Atta girl. That's the spark I used to see in you. You've got my full support on this, Helen. Whatever you have belongs to your heirs not Edward's girlfriend's offspring."

Helen moved quickly to the phone and caught Shirley just as she was about to leave the office.

"Helen, I'll get to work on this right away. I'm sure we can find a loophole somewhere. I'll get all the paperwork I can on it then call you back when I have something concrete."

"Shirley, I don't care how long it takes. She is not getting another penny from me. I don't care if she's a grandmother before this is all settled."

# Chapter Twenty-six

Gerald asked that Helen leave all the plans for the honeymoon cruise in his hands. He had travelled to Greece routinely during his years at sea and he wanted to surprise her with their tour destinations.

Guy was to be the best man and also offered to host an engagement party for the couple so the families could meet. There was a small entertainment room in his condo building and he arranged for a catered dinner on a weekend near the end of January. Nicholas was not able to attend. Ellie, Willis and their two children arrived the morning of the big day. Helen's three friends were invited as well. An old friend of Gerald's from Montreal, Bill Caron, also arrived with his wife, Yvonne.

The day before, Helen had accepted an offer on her condo with a closing date two weeks after they would arrive home from their honeymoon. Gerald had prepared a special dinner for them, complete with candles and a favourite wine. When they moved to the living room for dessert and coffee, he presented her with a small gift-wrapped parcel.

"Is this a memento for me for selling the condo?"

"No. I figured since we're attending our engagement party tomorrow night, we should be properly engaged."

Helen opened the parcel to find a ring with an emerald cut sapphire centred between two narrow rectangular cut diamonds in a platinum setting. Her birthstone for September protected by two of his for April. "I hope you like it, Helen. I had it designed especially for you."

He slid it on her finger and waited for her reply.

"Gerald, it's the most beautiful and unique ring I've ever seen."

"It had to be one of a kind, just like you, brown eyes."

"We're not teenagers, Gerald. I know you love me and I don't need a ring to feel engaged. Our promise of marriage is all the engagement necessary."

"You make me feel like a teenager, sweetheart. Besides we still have over two weeks before the wedding. I want every man around to know you're spoken for. I saw old Dave Belanger from the tenth floor giving you the once over at the mail boxes the other day. Pretty closely I might add."

Helen smiled. "He's so near-sighted, he probably had to get up close and personal to make sure I was a person and not a post. Poor old guy."

"Some of those old guys use their shortcomings as a ploy to gain the sympathy of unsuspecting younger women."

"Ha, ha. This younger woman was admiring his walker and thinking how much more useful it was compared to my crutches."

"One more week and you'll hopefully be free of them, my love. I know it's been a long haul for you, but you've done well with your therapy and with luck will walk down that aisle all on your own." He kissed the hand on which she wore the engagement ring. "Let's go celebrate our engagement."

"Now? Where do you want to go at this time of night?"

"The most exciting place in the neighbourhood. Our bedroom."

The dinner was prepared and served by the small catering business from Sparks Street. Guy and his girlfriend, Annie Nolan, were responsible for all the food and wine selections and decorated the room for the occasion.

Helen hoped no one would bring up the subject of Irene Urquhart. In fact she had warned her friends the topic was forbidden for the evening. She wanted to enjoy meeting and spending some time with Gerald's friends.

She had met Guy at lunch one day with Gerald and then he had visited her while she was recuperating. He was a clone of his father, however she learned his mother had also been blessed with dark brown eyes and hair, so it was possible he had a little of both in his looks. An educated and soft-spoken young man, his father was clearly proud of him. She learned then that he had met a young woman, Annie, who worked in an adjacent office in the building where he practiced and they managed to lunch together most days in the cafeteria.

Gerald had lots of stories to tell about Helen growing up. He focused on their elementary school years and skirted around the questions about their high school years and whether they had a romantic interest in each other during that time. Helen filled in some blanks about Gerald as a young a lad and did so with so such warmth and love in her eyes that everyone wondered what happened to this young couple who chose to take different paths. Before it could be questioned more deeply, Gerald changed the subject to tell about the places they were going to visit on their honeymoon.

Margaret asked about Gerald's sister and was told that Doreen was hoping to attend the wedding but had not been well lately. The woman was in her early fifties and worked as a nurse in Sault Area Hospital in Sault Ste. Marie, Ontario. Helen had been looking forward to meeting her and was disappointed when Doreen sent her regrets a few days before due to ill health.

No comments or questions had been forthcoming about the Irene Urquhart situation although everyone was dying to ask. Olivia had not been kind when told about the baby and petition but she knew better than to ruin a beautiful engagement party with any petty comments.

"Helen, I'm so happy you're staying in the building. Gerald won't mind letting us take over the apartment when it's your turn to host our bridge game?'

"He'll probably go spend the day at Guy's."

"Guy sure knows how to plan an event. Your engagement dinner last night was something else! He seems to be genuinely happy about you and his dad getting married."

"He told me he's never seen his dad so happy and he thanked me for making him so. It's wonderful going into a second marriage knowing that all the children are pleased with it. Both Nick and Ellie have given us their blessings as well. Ellie says she can't understand how I let him slip through my fingers in the first place."

"How did you?"

"It wasn't my doing. When we graduated from high school, he just up and left. No explanation. No good-bye. I was devastated. His mother couldn't or didn't shed any light on it either. I think she was as surprised as I was."

"Has he not given you a reason now, after all these years?"

"Not one that holds any weight."

"Well, the man obviously worships the ground you walk on so whatever his reasons, they are definitely a thing of the past. Just move forward and enjoy all the years ahead of you and don't look back."

Sarah had stopped by to see if Helen would sell her the bedroom suite in the guest room for her own apartment. Helen was planning on taking a few favourite pieces of furniture with her and Ellie had asked for some as well, but most of it was going to be auctioned off. She would be debt free when she walked through the door of Gerald's condo as Mrs. Gerald Mercier. It had been her goal and she would see it happen. With luck she would even have a little nest egg to tuck away for a rainy day. Unless Irene Urquhart got her hands on it. *No, don't go there, Helen. You are not going to allow that to happen."*

"I won't be looking back exactly, but I can't help a glance over my shoulder once in a while until we get Irene Urquhart finally and definitively out of my hair."

"Nothing happening on that front?"

"No. Shirley Simons is waiting for paperwork and then she'll go after DNA confirmation. However, I don't think Irene would be stupid enough to try something like this if the child wasn't Edward's."

"Well, let's get you married off and away on that dream cruise with your gorgeous groom. There'll be plenty of time to deal with law suits, babies and greedy mistresses when you come back. I hope your lawyer is able to shut her down once and for all."

"I just don't have a good feeling about all of this. Something seems off about it. If it's money she's after, I can't help but wonder why she didn't come after me when she first knew she was pregnant."

"She did call you, if I remember correctly. Maybe something happened that prevented her from following through until now."

"Yes, but what? That's what I'm concerned about. Why the delay and why now when I'm getting married and moving on?"

# Chapter Twenty-seven

At 3 p.m. on Saturday, February 14, Helen entered the front door of Notre Dame Cathedral on Sussex Street in downtown Ottawa. She proceeded up the aisle on the arm of her son, Nicholas. Walking slightly ahead of her was her daughter, Ellie, and waiting at the altar was Gerald and his son, Guy. Helen's grandchildren, her son-in-law and daughter-in-law, her three friends, Gerald's sister, Doreen and her daughter along with Gerald's friends from Montreal were ensconced in the pews within the sanctuary.

She wore a simple pale green suit and a strand of pearls that followed neatly the neckline of her suit. The small pearl grey clutch she carried was adorned with a single orchid. On her feet were pearl grey shoes with low heels to accommodate her still unsteady gait. Gerald looked dashing in his signature grey. A classic tailored suit with pale green shirt and slate green tie.

At 4 p.m. they exited the front door of the Cathedral into a sunny late afternoon sky. The temperature was a chilly -16 Celsius so the number of pictures were limited and they left for a reception at the Ottawa Marriott. Gerald and Helen had carefully selected a menu of hot and cold Hors d'oeuvres, desserts and a selection of both alcoholic and non-alcoholic drinks.

At 7 p.m. the last of the wedding guests left. Helen and Gerald went up to the dining room while their suite was cleaned from the reception and prepared for their wedding night. When they returned to their suite a couple of hours later, Helen was happy to remove her shoes and stretch her legs on the bed.

"I'm not as young as I used to be, Gerald. I hope you realize you have married a woman on the back side of fifty-five. I can probably form a real comradeship with some of those old women who complain about their aching bones and how they can predict a change in the weather."

"Helen, in case you haven't noticed, my calendar pages have been turning at the same rate as yours. To make any disparaging remarks about your age would only be self-deprecating. Besides, I hear older women make better lovers." He massaged her leg that had been broken in the accident and continued with her other leg. As his fingers caressed her foot, he bent to kiss her toes. "Why don't you let me pour you a bath so you can relax after a long day on your feet?"

"That sounds wonderful. I am dying to get into something more comfortable." She smiled as she recalled he had once referred to his bed as just that.

"Hmm. I like the sound of that."

He kissed each of her toes then went into the bathroom to draw her bath.

At 11 p.m. Gerald reached over and turned the bedside lamp off.

Nick, Rebecca and Benjamin were staying in Helen's condo for a few days. They had planned on having a short vacation in Ottawa before driving down to Kingston to spend another few days with Ellie and her family. They thought it was a wonderful idea for the young cousins to spend some time together.

Ellie's gang stopped at Helen's just long enough to pick up some of their belongings before driving home to Kingston, a two hour drive south and west, where Lake Ontario empties into the St. Lawrence River.

They were just carrying the last load down to their SUV when they heard Benjamin ask why the red light was flashing on Gramma's phone. No one had noticed it. Nick looked at Ellie and suggested it might be their mother leaving a message. Ellie went and clicked the voice mail to on. "Hi, Helen. It's Shirley Simons. I've heard from Ms. Urquhart's lawyer. There's a new development in the case. I can't remember when you are planning on leaving for your honeymoon but if you have a chance, give me a call before you go. Hope your wedding day went beautifully."

All the adults exchanged looks. "Should we call Mom?" Ellie asked the obvious question.

"Definitely not." Nick looked like he was ready to explode. "Mom is on her honeymoon."

"They're not leaving until tomorrow."

"This is their wedding night. They are officially on their honeymoon."

"Nick, what if it's something she should know about before she leaves."

"That bitch …"

"Watch your language in front of the children, Nick." Rebecca gave him a warning look.

"That … woman is not going to ruin Mom's wedding or honeymoon. Whatever it is can wait until she and Gerald get back."

"I understand how you feel but we can't let our feelings about Dad's mistress take precedence over a situation that isn't ours to make judgement on."

"Ellie, it's 8 o'clock on a Saturday night. Do you think Irene's lawyer is working tonight? I don't think so. Why upset Mom when that b— *woman* took over a year to bring it this far? You heard Mom. She doesn't care how long it takes, she's not giving in to any demands. So I don't see why this message can't sit here till Mom gets back."

"I suppose you're right, Nick. I'll just feel terrible if it's something urgent that Mom should have known about."

"I'll take responsibility for it if she gets upset about it but there's no reason she has to know we saw the message light tonight. Tomorrow she'll be on the plane." He gave his sister a hug and motioned her out the door. "We'll see you in a couple of days, Sis. Looking forward to spending a few days with you guys."

❣❣❣

They boarded a morning flight for Athens, Greece to start a two week honeymoon touring the Islands. Helen was surprised to learn they were staying in Athens for a short while, and then instead of boarding a regular tour ship, Gerald had arranged for a private yacht to take them island hopping. The owner of the boat was someone he knew. He had visited the islands many times when he was plying the international waters and he wanted to show Helen all his favourite places. Peter, the owner of the yacht, used to take him to quiet villages when he had a few days off and they had become friends.

"Cruise ships are for tourists, brown eyes. I hope you're not disappointed."

"Disappointed? How can I be disappointed with a romantic cruise on our own private yacht complete with a captain and crew bowing to our every command?"

"Good. I wanted you to enjoy these islands through the same eyes as I have over the years."

He wrapped her in his arms and spoke softly in her ear. "Whenever I came to these places I used to wonder if Helen would like this view. This bay? This sunset? My heart ached to bring you here, never dreaming it would actually happen." His eyes were moist as he brought her hand to his heart. "Do you know how much I love you, Helen? Have always loved you?"

"Gerald, I'm just so grateful that we found each other after all these years. I only pray God gives us many years to enjoy our life together."

"Do you want to have supper on the boat or on land this evening?" Carlo, the first mate, didn't realize until too late he had interrupted an intimate moment.

"Why don't we go to that restaurant on the other side of the island this evening? Maybe Peter will let Carlo have a night off in town."

Helen nodded her agreement.

They were seven days into their island hopping when Gerald decided he wanted go deep sea fishing to catch their evening meal. Helen begged off saying she would enjoy a day of reading and catching up on some mail. Gerald hired a small boat and its owner to take him out for three hours.

Helen was sipping a glass of iced tea and had just put her book down when Peter asked permission to join her.

"Gerald used to enjoy his fishing whenever he came to the islands. He said it was something most boys and young men did in his hometown but he never had the opportunity. I'm glad to see he's continuing to enjoy it in his later years."

"Gerald counts you among his friends, Peter. I can see why. You're a very caring person."

"Gerald is the best friend. He honours me by choosing my boat for the honeymoon, Mrs. Mercier."

"Please call me Helen."

"Of course, Mrs. Elene."

Helen smiled at the formality. "I thank you for the generosity of your time. You have the amazing ability to know what we want before we do. We just think we might want something and like magic, it's placed before us."

"I can never do enough for my friend. He saved the life of my son. Without his bravery I would have no son today. No grandson."

"I'm afraid I don't know about this. Gerald just said you were his friend, I'm not aware of your history."

"He never lets me bring it up. He is so modest."

"How did he save your son's life?"

"Twelve years ago, he was with me on this boat for maybe the second or third time. He and several friends from another island rented my yacht for a weekend. They wanted to play cards and get away from their work for a couple of days. The second evening out, a storm came up while the men were inside the salon playing cards. The water got rough and my son, Markos, who had eighteen years, was serving them. One of the men was drinking too much and getting louder and louder. He started to light a cigarette when Markos told him there is no smoking inside the boat. If he wants to smoke, he must go on deck.

"The man did not like being told what to do by someone so young. He told Markos he was paying well for the privilege of enjoying the boat ride and if he wanted to smoke, he would smoke. My son told him again he could not smoke inside. The man stood so quickly he knocked his chair over. He made a grab for Markos but before he could, Gerald pointed to a no smoking sign on the wall near the door and told him not to cause problems. The man was angry and made his way out on to the deck. When I saw someone walking on the deck, I called over the loudspeaker that it was dangerous on deck in this weather. When the man didn't go inside, I radioed Markos to go out and tell the man to come in."

Peter stopped and looked into the horizon.

"I didn't know there had been a situation. Gerald told me later that he noticed Markos hesitate after he had taken the call but he obeyed me and went out on the deck. Gerald followed him out in a few minutes and I saw the three of them arguing outside. Then the man pushed Markos. The deck was wet. He lost his footing and went overboard. The sea was too rough to see anything but Gerald didn't hesitate he threw a life line out, grabbed a preserver and jumped overboard when we caught a glimpse of Markos in the light from the boat.

They were out of sight for too long and I thought they were both drowned when the first mate noticed something in the water. We turned and dragged both of them into the boat. Markos was unconscious but First Mate Nick brought him around. No other man I have ever known would have jumped into black water like that — but Gerald did and today I still have a son. Whatever, that man wants and I can give him, it is his — for the rest of my life and my son's life also."

"He's never mentioned this."

"He never will and he told me twelve years ago that it is never to be mentioned again."

"Thank you for sharing it with me."

"He deserves for his wonderful lady to know she is married to a hero. Now it is my turn to say it is never to be mentioned again." With that Peter strode off and Helen didn't see him again until Gerald returned with a fine looking sea bream, looking mighty proud of himself.

"I caught our supper, Helen."

# Chapter Twenty-eight

"It's good to be home."

Gerald smiled as he stooped and rubbed his back.

"I said it's good … Gerald, what's the matter?"

"I should have realized you would have put on five or six pounds during our trip before I carried you over the threshold."

She swatted him in the arm before leaning in and kissing him. "I told you I shouldn't have eaten those rich desserts you kept pushing on me every night."

"It *is* good to be home." He clicked the television on and switched it to the news channel. "I guess we'll find out how good. I'll take this luggage cart back downstairs before I get too comfortable."

Before the wedding he had moved some of his things to the spare bedroom closet and wardrobe to make room for Helen's clothes in the walk-in closet. After the luggage was unpacked and Helen had laundry going in the washer, she sat and accepted a mixed drink from Gerald.

"It feels good to be doing something domestic." She clinked her glass against his.

"Did you want to go down and check on your place, Helen?"

"It can wait until morning. I just want to enjoy being home. Maybe we can have some Chinese or a pizza delivered." She put her feet up on the ottoman. "Tomorrow, I'll work myself into a routine. Tonight I just want to sit and enjoy my memories."

"Our memories."

"Our memories. I can hardly wait to upload our pictures into the computer and print some of them. It's hard to believe we've been married two and a half weeks. Our honeymoon went by so quickly."

"You're an old married woman already."

"You're right. Figuratively and literally."

"Does the sisterhood know we were coming back tonight?"

"They know. You better hang a tie over the door knob so they know not to come in."

"Ha, ha, Helen. Are we really going to need a signal?"

"Not really. They'll respect our privacy." She smiled when she remembered the ups and downs of the relationship between Gerald and her three friends. It had been a real roller coaster ride and poor Stella had been caught in the middle of it.

"Tomorrow I'll go down and check the phone for messages too."

"You can do that from here, Helen."

"No. I'm still on my honeymoon. Tomorrow the happily ever after starts."

With that the phone rang. Gerald picked it up and said hello.

"Grandpa? Is that you?"

Gerald held the phone for a minute, not knowing what to say.

"Andy?"

"Yes. I asked my mom if it would be okay if I called you grandpa now but she said to get your permission first. Is it okay, Grandpa?"

"Of course it's okay. It's better than okay. In fact I insist on it." His lip quivered as he spoke.

"He said it's better than okay, Mom. He insists on it." Gerald could hear the muffle as Andy half covered the phone.

Helen asked who it was and Gerald mouthed "My grandson, Andy."

Startled, she asked if Andy wanted to speak to her. Gerald shrugged his shoulders.

"So you're home now? Did you have a good honeymoon, Grandpa? Did you go on one of those big ships?"

Gerald laughed at the barrage of questions. "Yes, we are. Yes, we did. And no, we didn't. We toured around on a much smaller boat that belonged to a friend of mine."

"Bummer. I thought you were going on one of those big ones with swimming pools and water slides and stuff."

Gerald laughed. "Well, your grandmother forgot her bathing suit so we thought we'd better not waste our money on swimming pool ships."

"Oh. I guess you didn't think about going to the department store and buying her one. That's what Mom does when we forget ours."

"I guess your mom is a quicker thinker than we are."

"Can I talk to Grandma now or is she at her apartment?"

"She's right here and I'm sure she would be happy to talk to you."

"Okay. I love you, Grandpa, bye."

Gerald hesitated again, "I love you too, Andy. Take care, young fella."

As he gave the phone to Helen, he told her he was going to the Chinese restaurant a few doors down the street. She was already chatting and laughing with her family, when he let himself out the door.

Gerald hadn't returned when Helen completed her conversation so she called her friends to let them know she was home. She promised when all the pictures were uploaded, they would be invited to a Greek slide show evening. She contemplated checking her messages on her home phone but decided against it. If there was anything urgent about the sale of her home there was nothing she could do about it before morning anyway. Two more weeks and she would be free of everything connected to her and Edward.

After searching for her comfortable slippers and her hair dryer, she realized the only things in her new home were basically what she had taken on her honeymoon and few newer outfits she had purchased shortly before her wedding.

"Damn, I guess I have to run down to the old place after all." She grabbed her keys, left a note for Gerald and quickly went to the elevator.

Helen looked around the mostly empty apartment. Some of her furniture had been sold and the balance would be moved into Gerald's place, her new home. Ellie had arranged for movers to transport the furniture she was taking to her place and offered to store some for Nicholas as well in her basement. He had insisted there were some pieces that had fond memories for him and someday when they permanently settled into a home, he would send for them.

The blinking light on the phone caught Helen's eye but she ignored it. She found her slippers, her hair dryer and a few other things that would fit in the bag she found and started for the door. Once again her eyes were drawn to the flashing light. She went over and looked at the message panel and saw there were five messages.

*Oh, what the heck. I may as well see who tried to reach me. I'll listen to them and deal with them tomorrow.*

She deleted the first two which were of no interest, listened to the third, and then the fourth. She never did get to the fifth.

Gerald returned with two bags of his and Helen's favourite Chinese dishes. He set the kitchen table with plates and cutlery.

"Soup's on, Helen." He called toward the bedroom hallway assuming she was folding laundry.

When she didn't respond after several minutes he went to look for her. He checked every room before he noticed the note on the table by his recliner. After another fifteen minutes had gone by, he called her apartment. No response. *She must be on her way up.*

Fifteen more minutes passed and he called again. No response. He was just about to check on her when he heard the door open and close.

"Helen, you look like you've seen a ghost."

She walked into the kitchen like a zombie.

"Sit down, love. What is it?" He pulled a chair out and helped her sit.

"What's the matter? Are you ill?"

"Yes, Gerald, I am. I'm damn good and sick. I … I … Damn. Pull up my messages and listen for yourself."

He quickly asked for her password, dialled her old number and the messages came on one by one. He listened to them all and found the last one was a telemarketer.

"Helen, we have to talk to Shirley tomorrow. Will she answer her phone if you call her tonight?"

"I'm not ready to talk to her. I have to think." She stood up so quickly she knocked the chair over.

"Damn that woman. Damn Edward. Damn them both to hell! They continue to screw me even in death. First he dies and leaves me penniless. Now she dies and leaves me a child to support? No bloody way!"

# Chapter Twenty-nine

"Helen, we *must* talk to Shirley." Gerald had walked a distraught Helen to the sofa and was rubbing her arm. All thoughts of a Chinese dinner had vanished. She was nursing a stiff drink instead.

"You're 57 years old. There is no way you can be expected to care for an infant. I will call Shirley and set up an appointment for late tomorrow. That will give you time to take this all in and prepare some questions. We don't even know if you're legally responsible for the financial burden of this child."

"I thought that was going to be the least of my worries, child support. I didn't know she was going to ask that we raise the child, for heaven's sake. He's Edward's bastard. He's no responsibility of mine. How presumptuous of that home wrecker to think for one minute that I would want her baby in my house!" She started to laugh. "Gerald, this is a joke. It's got to be a sick joke. How can my lawyer even think I would agree to such a thing? It's ridiculous, absolutely ridiculous!"

She was becoming hysterical.

"Calm down, love. Of course, it's ridiculous. We'll go to Shirley's office tomorrow and she'll tell us just how crazy this woman's scheme is."

❣❣❣

"Irene Urquhart's scheme actually isn't that crazy. We could go back through current history all the way to medieval times and find countless situations where bastards have been raised by the first family. This especially holds true when there are siblings to the child involved."

Helen paled and grasped for Gerald's hand.

"*Have* been raised but not necessarily *must* be raised."

"Of course. Unfortunately, Edward's child with Irene may have legal claim to his estate. We can pursue this through the court system if you choose. Irene was clever enough to name you as the chosen legal guardian so you will have the option of deciding who will ultimately raise the child. You can place him for adoption, you can make him a ward of the court, or you can raise him within your own family. Other than the assets belonging to you and Edward, he will never have legal claim against any assets that belong to you and Gerald."

"I don't want to raise him. I don't even want to see him." Helen was voicing her feelings with determination.

"Do you not want to discuss this with the child's siblings before making a decision? They are, after all, his natural half-sister and half-brother. They may want a say in the matter."

Helen shook her head. "They won't want anything to do with him either."

"Are you positive, Helen?" Gerald spoke for the first time.

"Why would they want to? This child is the result of their father's infidelity.

"He is still their blood relation. Have you told them about this situation, Helen?" Shirley could sense defiance in Helen's tone of voice.

"No. I didn't see any point."

"The point is they may see this differently. The child is an innocent victim in all of this. He may challenge his birthright when he is old enough to do so but for now he is just a baby who has had the misfortune to lose both his parents. He does have siblings who are of legal age who may like to be part of the decision making process for his future."

"Helen, love, give it a little thought. It wouldn't hurt to let Ellie and Nick know about Irene's request. Even if they agree with you, they may resent not having been informed and allowed to be a part of the decision. They do know about the baby after all so it won't be a complete shock to them."

Shirley stood. "I think you should take a week or so to think about this before making a final decision, Helen. Sometimes talking to a parish priest can help. The baby is in the care of a foster family right now and will remain there until a permanent home is established. There are many good families out there looking to adopt so placing the child will be no problem. Don't make a hasty decision."

❣❣❣

"Absolutely not! My father and that red-headed bitch ruined our family. He lied rather than spend time with his grandchildren and now we're supposed to be all gaga about raising their bastard? Not on your life." Nicholas was shouting into the phone.

Helen tried to calm him. "I'm only asking because you and the baby share the same father. He is your half-brother, Nicholas. My lawyer, as well as Gerald and I, thought you and Ellie should have some input in the decision."

"Well, you now have my answer, Mom. I want nothing to do with that woman's child."

Ellie was remaining silent. Helen had to ask her to speak so they could be certain the three-way connection was intact.

"I really need to think about this, Mom. My first reaction was the same as Nick's. Dad hurt us all so badly I still find it hard to forgive him. However, I can't help thinking that the baby is my half-brother. I need time to think about him going to a completely unknown family and never having contact with him."

Nick gasped. "Ellie, you can't be serious. What are you thinking about? Mom can't raise him so there is no choice but to place him for adoption. He is innocent of his parents' wrongdoing and deserves to be in a family where there is no resentment. I don't think I could look at him without being reminded of Dad's deceit and the nerve of that Urquhart woman to even presume we would accept her baby."

"Their baby, Nick. Not hers. Theirs. Dad's blood is in his veins too. Can you really overlook that?"

"Yes."

"I can't."

"Ellie, what are you saying?" Helen couldn't believe what she was hearing.

"I'm saying I need time to think about this. I need some time, Mom. I'll probably agree with you and Nick but I just need time to think clearly. Can I call you back tomorrow?"

"Yes, of course, darling. I would hate for you to think you made an important decision in haste."

"Ellie, you're out of your mind. How can you even consider any other decision than letting Mom place him for adoption?"

"Nick, I need time. Don't push me. I'll call you tomorrow, Mom."

They could hear the click as Ellie broke the connection.

"Mom, why didn't you just go ahead and sign adoption papers? It would have been out of our hair and you could get on with your life."

"This seemed like a good idea at the time, Nick."

"It was a lousy idea."

"Not if your sister has such strong feelings about it. I wouldn't have been able to forgive myself if she had found out later and hated me for it. I'm sure she'll agree with us once she's had a chance to weigh all the options and see that it's best for the baby. I'll talk to you tomorrow, Nicholas."

Gerald had his arms out for a bear hug. Helen gladly went into the warm, strong circle of his love.

"Is it ever going to end, Gerald? Are we ever going to enjoy some peace and happiness? A year and a half later and Edward's ghost is still among us stirring up trouble. You may grow tired of it all and wish we had never met again."

"On the contrary. I'm so glad I'm here and able to offer a shoulder, if nothing else. I hate to even think about you going through this on your own." He smiled and held her an arm's length away. "What am I saying? You would have had the sisterhood to help you solve the problem. Lord knows, they may have given you better advice than I. Nicholas certainly didn't like the idea of being drawn into it."

"He's more like his father in some ways than he cares to admit. Edward always preferred I take care of family matters. Of course that left him free to deal with matters outside the home."

"Speaking of the sisterhood, have you seen them since we returned?"

"No. I had promised I would get our pictures all sorted and uploaded into a slide show we could all watch. It went completely out of my head."

"Why don't you work on that? It will give you something to do while Ellie thinks over her answer. Maybe we could invite the girls over for dinner tomorrow. I'll cook and you visit."

They hadn't heard from Ellie the next day and Helen didn't want to push her. She spent her time sorting and cropping, subtitling and arranging all her pictures in an electronic album. All was ready when her three friends arrived mid-afternoon. Gerald mixed drinks and heated canapés while the women caught up on condo gossip. He was pleased that none of it seemed to involve Stella Jacobson.

Finally, it was show time and Helen began the picture presentation. She had been meticulous in her picture taking, making sure that each scene and event had been properly recorded as to location, time and names of persons in each. A couple of postcards had preceded the honeymooners' return so they were not surprised there was no huge cruise ship. They all agreed this appeared to be much more intimate and romantic. Gerald was able to give them a history and some local folklore about each island and village. He had personal stories about many of the people in several locations. Helen would have loved to share the story of Gerald's heroism in saving the life of their captain's son but she had made a promise.

Gerald went in to the kitchen to put the finishing touches on the meal he had prepared. The ladies eventually were seated at the dining table and Gerald poured wine for all. He had prepared a fish dinner similar to one they had experienced on the yacht one evening. Of course the fish was a different species but it was a pretty good substitute. He cheated for dessert and served pastries purchased at a Greek deli in the neighbourhood. Dessert was accompanied by several choices of liqueurs. Margaret, too frightened to try ouzo before dinner, decided to taste it with dessert. She found she enjoyed the liquorice flavour and asked for a second. Gerald warned her about the slow reaction to the high alcohol count but she was determined to have another.

"Please don't phone me in the morning, Margaret. I won't be held responsible for your hangover."

"I've never been drunk in my life. I don't think two drinks are going to make me drunk now."

"We'll see."

"Helen, when will you be ready to play bridge again? It's been awhile since you've played." Sarah offered to host the next game at her place. Helen checked her calendar and it was set up for three days later. The women thanked Gerald for the Greek dinner and Helen for the slide show and left.

After the kitchen was clean and the dishwasher loaded, Helen glanced at the clock.

"Are you thinking about Ellie?" Gerald always seemed to read her mind.

"The thought had crossed my mind but I'm not sure I want to hear what she has to say. I keep thinking that she would have called by now if she decided to agree with Nicholas and me. Gerald, I don't know what I'll do if she feels strongly that the baby should be kept in the family."

"Do you really think she might?"

"Why else hasn't she called?"

Just then the phone rang. Helen hurried to it, and had mixed feelings about not recognizing the phone number on the display screen before picking it up. "Hello?"

"Helen, this is Marcie, Doreen's daughter. Is Uncle Gerald there, please?"

"Yes, of course, Marcie. Just a moment." She handed the phone to her husband.

"Hi, Marcie. How are you?"

"I'm fine, Uncle, but my mother is not doing so well. In fact, she was hoping you were home from your honeymoon. She'd like you to come here if you can."

"What's happened, Marcie? She seemed to be fine at the wedding."

"She was sicker than she let on because she didn't want your wedding ruined. She's had cancer for quite some time and I guess her latest round of treatment has really knocked her legs out from under her. Can you come? She … she says she wants to see you one last time." Her voice broke and Gerald heard her soft sobs which she tried to hide. "Oh, Uncle Gerald, I'm so sorry for ruining your return home.

"I'll be there as soon as we can get a flight. If none are available, we'll drive. Let me see what I can do and I'll call you back, Marcie."

He quickly explained the situation to Helen and then looked up the airline number. There was a flight leaving at 7 a.m. the next morning.

# Chapter Thirty

By 5:30 a.m. Guy, who had insisted on driving them to the airport, was outside 73 Windsor stowing their luggage in the back of his SUV. "Make sure you give Aunt Doreen my love, Dad. She's always been so good to me, treated me like her own son. After Mom died, we became quite close."

"I will, Son. Hopefully, this isn't the end but I guess we have to be prepared. I sure as hell am not ready to say good-bye to her. She's always been the one so full of life."

"I know, Dad. I feel sorry for Marcie, too. She wanted so badly to make Auntie Doreen a grandmother but it just never happened."

"She's young yet but I know it might be too late for Doreen. We better get moving. This snow is hard to take after the warm temperatures we've just come home from. I hope the plane takes off on time."

They gradually flew out of the snow as the plane headed west and by the time they approached the airport in Sault Ste. Marie the skies were clear. Lake Superior was still frozen as they circled around to approach the runway. Gerald rented a car rather than take a taxi. It was about a half hour drive into town but he knew he'd probably regret not having a vehicle if he didn't rent one. He chose a good size SUV with winter tires. In Sault Ste. Marie, winter storms could whip up at any time bringing drifting snow with them, even in March.

Doreen was at the hospital on the Great Northern Road, part

of Highway 17 which headed north and west around Lake Superior to Thunder Bay. It was a brand new hospital just a couple of years old. They decided to drive directly to the hospital before coming back to check in at the Fairfield Inn. She was sound asleep when they arrived.

Gerald felt the swift kick to his gut when he saw how emaciated she was. How had they not noticed when she came for the wedding? She shouldn't have come. It probably took a lot out of her. The bruises under her eyes went half way down her cheeks. Her teeth seemed too big for her mouth and her hair was patches of fine fuzz. Helen slid her arm across his back. "Jesus, Helen. Dear Lord, Jesus. How did she travel and look so healthy just a few weeks ago?"

They sat with her for an hour before Helen suggested she would stay with her while Gerald checked them into the hotel and grabbed something to eat. He called Marcie before he left to let her know they had arrived. She worked at an insurance office downtown and promised to come by during her lunch break.

Marcie and Gerald came through the door together. With conversation and increased noise in the room, Doreen stirred and looked around.

"Gerald. You came." A wan smile gave a brief light to her eyes before they glazed over and closed once more. She motioned weakly with her hand for him to come closer.

Marcie caught Helen's eye and pointed to the door. They slipped outside and left brother and sister alone.

"I think she's just been hanging on waiting for her big brother to come. She's always idolized Uncle Gerald."

"Let's go grab a coffee and you have a sandwich, Marcie. We'll give them a little time alone."

"You are so understanding, Helen. I guess I should call you Aunt Helen."

"Helen is fine unless it makes you feel better to call me aunt.

I never had any siblings so I don't have any nieces or nephews. My first husband was an only child as well."

"You got married here I understand. Did you know your husband from work?"

"No, we were introduced at a wedding reception. It was kind of arranged without me knowing." She smiled. "I guess that sounds kind of old-fashioned."

"Was that after my uncle left town?"

"Yes, he was long gone by then. He left right after high school."

"Oh, that's right too. I understand you tried to find him when he left."

"It took me a long time to forgive him for deserting me. I was devastated." She sat back in her chair and looked at Gerald's niece. "Your uncle was quite a charmer, even back then. I thought we were going to get right serious when we finished high school. It didn't work out that way."

"Were you angry with your father for interfering?"

"What?"

"Your father. You must have been upset with him when he told my uncle to get out of town."

"What are you talking about?"

Marcie immediately flushed with embarrassment. "You didn't know. I mean … I thought … oh, no. Oh no. I'm sorry. I must have misunderstood. I … forget what I said. I'm sorry."

She started to get up but Helen took her arm and asked her to sit back down.

"You've started something that I think you better finish." Her voice was tense and her tone even more so.

"You're angry with me. I don't blame you."

"Marcie, I'm not angry with you. Obviously, you thought I knew something that I didn't. Now finish what you were saying."

"Oh, God. Mom will kill me and so will Uncle Gerald. I swear, I thought you knew."

"Knew what?"

Marcie looked around the room for an escape but none offered itself. She didn't want to hurt this woman who she thought had known all along how her father had treated Gerald.

"I'm waiting. You better spill it before your uncle shows up."

"Whenever Uncle Gerald came for a visit or we went to Montreal, Mom used to shake her head and tell me how sad it was that Uncle's life was wasted because of your father."

"What did she mean by that?"

"Well, my grandmother …" She started to cry. "Oh God, I can't. My poor grandmother."

"What has your grandmother to do with this?"

"I can't. I … I just can't." Marcie ran from the cafeteria.

Helen remained sitting. She didn't know quite what to make of what had just transpired. Obviously, Gerald and his mother had been hurt by her own father. But how? Why would her father tell Gerald to get out of town? Should she ask him? Why hadn't Gerald told her? What was the big secret? "Well, he's got enough on his plate with Doreen. I'm not about to add more. Right now anyway." She realized she had spoken out loud and looked around but no one had heard her.

Gerald was alone with Doreen when she came back to the room. She had gone outside and walked around the parking lot for a little while thinking to give Marcie time with her mother.

"How's she doing? Did she wake up at all?

"Not really. Her breathing is pretty shallow. I'm quite concerned. I was hoping Marcie would come back up but I guess the two of you must have had a good visit over lunch."

Helen didn't do much more than nod, then she smiled at Doreen. "Hello again, my little sister-in-law."

Gerald turned to see that Doreen's eyes were wide open. "Did you have a good sleep, sis?"

She took Gerald's offered hand and kissed it. "I'm sorry. I'm not being a very good hostess. I asked you to come here and then I can't stay awake."

"You obviously need your sleep. How long have you been in here?"

"I'm not sure. A few days maybe."

"Why did you come to Ottawa, Doreen? You obviously weren't well. Helen and I would have understood."

"I wanted to see you two finally together." She smiled at Helen. "You two have been apart for too long. You've loved each other since you were teenagers."

Helen knelt beside the bed. "Doreen, all you had to do was ask and we would have come to you. We could have left for our honeymoon from here just as easily."

"No. I wanted to see you actually get married. When I see my mother again I wanted to able to tell her that Gerald and Helen are married. Church wedding and all just like we had always hoped for."

Helen started to cry. "I had no idea."

"It broke us up to see Gerald so unhappy. Finally he quit coming home at all because he couldn't bear looking across at your house."

"That's enough, Doreen." Gerald patted her hand. "We're here now and when you get out of here, we'll take you out and make up for lost time."

"I won't be getting out of here, Gerald. We all know that. I'm just happy to see you one more time. My big brother. My big sister." She looked at Helen. "I've never had a sister before."

"Nor did I. We have that in common."

"We both love the same man. We have that in common too. Since my Dave died, Gerald has been the only man in my life."

"You were a very young widow, Doreen. You raised Marcie all on your own and you've done a great job. I'm looking forward to getting to know her better."

"Poor Marcie. She wanted to give me a grandchild in the worst way. Maybe someday her prayers for a baby will be answered."

"She's young yet with a good number of child bearing years ahead of her. Has she been married long?

"Eleven years. The doctor told her it isn't going to happen but she keeps hoping."

Gerald joined in. "Sometimes when you least expect it, a miracle happens and your prayers are answered."

Doreen noticed the look he turned in his wife's direction. He most of all, understood about miracles happening when you least expect them. "Gerald, you will keep in touch with her, won't you? She adores you."

"Of course I will, Doreen. All that husband of hers knows about is computers. When she does get around to having a baby I'll have to teach it all the outdoors stuff. I'll be the little one's great-uncle for Pete's sake."

Doreen's eyes were getting heavy again. "Give me a kiss and get out of here. Let me get some rest."

Gerald leaned over and gave his sister a soft kiss on the lips and another on her forehead. "I love you, little sister."

"I love you too, big brother." It was barely more than a whisper.

She hung on for two more days before her body finally started shutting down. Doreen had made it known she never wanted to be kept alive by artificial means. When the end came it was fast. She was breathing one minute and the next minute not. Her body was cremated and they had a celebration of life at the church she had attended all her life. Helen was amazed by how full the church was but Doreen was well known and respected. A quiet woman, she loved her family above all else.

Helen never had another opportunity to talk to Marcie alone. When she helped the young woman go through Doreen's things Gerald was close by and Marcie certainly wasn't going to discuss Helen's father and Gerald's mother in front of him. They stayed for several days after the funeral and left for home with Gerald, the executor of her estate, promising to return to settle some legal matters in another month or so.

When Helen was finishing packing her bag at the hotel, Marcie pulled up as Gerald was leaving to get the car washed. She only stayed long enough to give Helen a well-worn blue diary-type note book. "I was hoping I would get a chance to see you alone. Put this in your bag and don't read it in front of Uncle Gerald." She gave Helen a warm, lingering hug. "I hope you and my uncle have as many years together as you had apart."

As she reached the door, she turned. "I love you, Auntie Helen." Then hurried out.

# Chapter Thirty-one

Helen stared at the book off and on for two weeks. It sat in her lingerie drawer where she lifted the cover, peeking inside once in a while. She was curious. She was frightened. She knew it contained things she me be sorry knowing.

It had been a difficult two weeks. They had arrived home to find that Ellie and Nicholas were at loggerheads. She did not want their father's baby to be made a ward of the courts and Nicholas was refusing to support her decision. They had been back and forth over the issue since first learning of Irene's death. In the interim, Helen had told her friends about the situation and of course their words about Irene were not kind. No one had seen the baby and he was never referred to by name. Helen knew she had to be the one to make a decision and it would have to be soon. She had been paying for the baby's care since she officially became the baby's custodian and had asked her lawyer to find foster parents to care for the child. It had to end. Shirley had been patient during Gerald's family ordeal but now it was time to resolve the issue.

"Helen, you can't seriously be thinking about raising this child!" Sarah was dumbfounded.

"You're 57 years old for heaven's sake. Gerald is at least as old as you. You're going to ask him to raise your former husband's child when you should be enjoying your time with each other after all these years? You have grandchildren older than this baby." Olivia stood open-mouthed.

Helen looked from one to the other. "I'm just saying that Ellie feels so strongly about keeping him within the family. She feels he's her baby brother and hates the thought of losing touch with him."

"Then let her raise him!" Sarah took Helen by the shoulders. "It shouldn't have gone this far. Helen, you just found happiness and independence with a man who absolutely adores you and God knows how much you love him. Do you want to risk that? I'm sorry, I love Ellie like my own daughter, but she is being a little selfish here."

"The baby is her brother, after all. They have the same blood flowing through their veins. I'm not sure I should be so quick to wrench them apart." She shrugged off Sarah's grip and slouched onto Olivia's sofa.

"There may be another solution."

The three women turned when Stella, who had been sitting quietly taking the conversation in, rose from her chair and came to sit by Helen. She had already been in Olivia's apartment going over the finances from the registry she now owned when Helen and Sarah arrived. Helen's friends were surprised when they had found Stella to be a likable, warm woman. They respected the ideas and changes she brought to the business she had purchased from Helen. Olivia had even invited her to fill in at bridge while Helen was away on her honeymoon. She had remained silent while Helen's dilemma was being discussed.

"Helen you told us the other day about Gerald's niece who wants a baby desperately and probably will never conceive. Maybe she and her husband would consider adopting this child?"

Four sets of eyes stared at her.

"Stella, you are so perceptive. It's an idea certainly worth considering. I know Marcie and Kevin would be excellent parents and it might satisfy Ellie's need to know the baby is well cared for and almost family." Helen smiled for the first time in weeks. "I'm going upstairs right now and talk to Gerald about it." She took Stella's hands in hers. "Thank you so, so much."

Helen hadn't told her friends earlier about this latest development. At first she was stunned at being forced into a situation of becoming legal custodian of the love child of her late husband and his mistress. How often does that happen to someone? Then there had been the rush trip to Sault Ste. Marie when Doreen needed them.

She learned through her own lawyer and Irene Urquhart's that the phone call she had received from the woman the previous summer had been intended to tell her about the pregnancy and imminent birth. Irene had in fact been hoping that Helen might find it in her heart to help with some child support. She had told her lawyer that it seemed a reasonable request since the baby would be Edward's child and that he should legally be entitled to the same support and proceeds from the estate as the other two children. When Helen hung up on her and mentioned lawyer, she dragged her feet and did not immediately follow through. It wasn't until she was diagnosed with breast cancer immediately following the baby's birth when an abnormality was discovered during breast feeding that she thought again about ensuring her baby's future. A biopsy confirmed the tumour was an aggressive form of malignancy and a mastectomy was followed up with chemotherapy. She was on maternity leave from her job which enabled her to care for the baby with minimal help from a friend. When the cancer spread to her other breast and another tumour found in a lung, she sought legal advice once again and started proceedings to make Edward's family responsible for his child. She died while Helen and Gerald were away on their honeymoon and since there was no other known family, the infant was placed in foster care pending the result of the current legal proceedings. Since Helen had never agreed to guardianship, she could not legally be held responsible. The fact that Ellie had concerns about the baby, however, placed Helen in a position of having to consider an alternative to washing her hands of the matter. Stella's idea just might be the ideal solution.

Gerald ran a hand through his hair as he contemplated the suggestion. Helen was a bundle of excited nerves even thinking there could be such a simple resolution to a complex problem.

"Helen, we don't even know if Marcie and Kevin would be open to the idea of adoption, let alone a baby that has strong blood ties to your family."

"I don't understand why family ties would be a bad thing. I would think that would be a plus."

"Do you not think she may be intimidated by the fact that her baby is a brother to your children? She may feel like she's being watched or even judged whatever decisions she and Kevin make raising the baby. She may feel like the child is never really hers — that she's just a … a … I don't know, a chosen caregiver maybe."

"I really don't see why that would be the case."

"I'm leaving Nicholas out of the equation because he obviously doesn't feel the connection Ellie does. However, this being their sibling, their brother, do you think Ellie might not feel a little possessive? Want to keep an eye on things to make sure her little brother is well taken care of? I think it's only human nature and Ellie may not even realize she's doing it. Then from Marcie's point of view she may feel that she's being scrutinized even if she's not."

"I hadn't thought about it like that. You may be right." Helen looked perplexed. "However, I do think the opportunity should be presented to Marcie and Kevin and let them decide if they're even interested in adoption and whether it's even legally possible. I don't know if arm's length comes in to play in this type of circumstance."

Helen and Gerald broached the idea to Helen's lawyer to discuss legalities and then called Marcie to arrange a short visit. They decided to drive to Sault Ste. Marie as the long range weather forecast looked promising.

They stopped in Blind River to have dinner and a young family came in with a toddler in tow. An elderly man, supposedly the child's grandfather came in later and took a seat with them. The child's eyes lit up as the older man crouched down and started tugging on the baby's shoeless toes.

Helen watched Gerald smiling at the family. "I remember you telling Doreen that you would have to teach Marcie and Kevin's child how to do all the outdoor things when the time came. Will it make a difference to you if they choose *this* child to be their own?"

"Why would it?"

"It's Ed's son."

"Edward is dead. He died not even knowing he was going to be a father again. Irene is dead. This child is no one's son until someone adopts him. If it's Marcie and Kevin, then he will be their son and my grand-nephew and yours. That's the only relationship he will have to either of us."

Helen looked at the family again when the toddler started to giggle loudly. She felt Gerald's hand on hers. "I hope Marcie does adopt him." He winked at her.

It took Marcie and Kevin only a week to contact Shirley Simons and make arrangements to see the baby. It was love at first sight. Before the end of April the little red-headed infant was on a plane on his way to his new home in Sault Ste. Marie. In mid-June, Ellie and Willis drove west with their children to stand as godparents for David Gerald McAffrey.

Great-uncle Gerald and Great-aunt Helen looked on.

# Chapter Thirty-two

Gerald had gone to play golf with a fellow golfer from their church. The other man had lived in Richmond before retiring and buying a condo downtown. The two men always made a day of it by going out to the Richmond Centennial Golf Course where they enjoyed eighteen holes in a quiet semi-rural setting. The green fees were reasonable, the fairways and putting greens well maintained and the beer cold.

Helen was at loose ends and decided to see what the shelves had to offer in a book store a block over from Windsor. While digging through her dresser drawer searching for a pair of anklets to slip on inside her track shoes, her fingers came to rest on a leather journal. She opened it and took a quick shuffle through the pages. Not sure about the wisdom of opening that can of worms, she threw the book on the bed and finished putting on her shoes.

She hesitated, then slid her hand across the duvet and picked up the journal. What would she find? Marcie gave it to her for a reason. Was there something inside that would explain Marcie's reference to Gerald's mother and her own dad?

*Don't be a coward, Helen. You know you're curious.*

She settled in a comfortable chair in the den after placing a cup of chai tea on the lamp table beside it. The natural light that came through the bay window made this her favourite spot for reading. Inside the front cover was an inscription indicating this had been a gift from Gerald for Doreen's eleventh birthday.

The text was written in neat cursive in various shades of ink. The notations started out tentative some no longer than a sentence or two, some filling a page and a half. It was evident Doreen had been reluctant to share her innermost thoughts and feelings in the beginning but as Helen turned the pages, the entries became more intimate. Feeling almost like a voyeur Helen was reluctant to do more than skim most of the notes. Doreen's devotion to Gerald was evident from the very beginning. She held him in high esteem. He was her hero. His odd jobs that he had while in high school provided her with the extras that most preteens deemed necessary to be popular and win friends. Apparently it was Gerald and their older brother, Joseph, who helped with groceries and who brought the special treats home on paydays.

Some of this Helen already knew. She remembered helping him pick out gifts for Doreen on special occasions. She had envied him having siblings. There always seemed to be so much laughter and joy at their house. She put the journal down and refreshed her tea.

About a third of the way through the book, the tone changed. Doreen was concerned there was something wrong with Gerald. He no longer joked with her and quit teasing her about having boyfriends. He worked longer hours and didn't seem to care about school anymore. He spent more and more time away from home. Her notes indicated his mother was worried too. Then the day of graduation came and instead of being excited he was "sombre" as Doreen expressed it. She and her mother attended the exercises. Joe was away working on job in another town. He was an apprentice for an electrical company and was required to take work out of town quite often.

Helen's tea got cold as she read. She stiffened when she came to a page that made her blood run cold. How could Doreen write such horrible things about her father? She put the book down for a moment before continuing on. Eventually, the denial faded and was replaced with the absolute fury Gerald must have felt. She dropped the book and buried her face in her hands.

❣❣❣

Gerald arrived home exhilarated from his excellent round of golf. The day had been sunny with just enough breeze to keep the temperature comfortable but not strong enough to affect the drives on the long fairways. He entered the living room and saw Helen in the den in her favourite chair. As he approached he noticed the dried tears on her cheeks.

He knelt in front of her and tapped her arm. "What's the matter, love? Did you get some bad news or something?"

She stirred. "Oh, Gerald." She seemed almost reluctant to wake up.

"What is it, Helen?"

The tears started again. He took her hands and eased her up so he could hold her in a bear hug. "Tell me. What's the matter?"

She looked around and spotted the journal on the floor. Gerald saw it at the same time and picked it up. He opened it and knew immediately what had his wife so upset.

"How did you get this?"

"It doesn't matter how I got it. I finally know the truth. The truth you should have told me forty years ago."

"I couldn't. You can see that."

"I hate him. How could the father I always loved and cherished have been such a monster? My mother had to have known. How and why could she have allowed this to happen?"

"She never knew. She's blameless, Helen. Your mother was a sweet woman who loved you. She even asked my mother one time why I went away so quickly and didn't come back."

Helen took his face in both her hands. "I am so, so sorry."

"There is no reason for you to apologize. This was between your father and me."

"I'm surprised Doreen could be so polite to me whenever I saw her. She seemed genuinely happy when we were married. She should have hated me. Hated my family. Because of us she was deprived of her big brother. She suffered her mother's loneliness after you left."

"Doreen knew how much I loved you. She always sensed you had feelings for me too. She told me how you used to ask about my travels and why I never came home. She knew."

"God, Gerald. All this time wasted. All these years gone thanks to that controlling, selfish bastard."

"He was only behaving like a father, Helen, protecting his daughter."

"Bullshit! Your mother tried her best to give her children a good home with clean clothes and nourishing food on the table. She was a good mother, Gerald. I used to envy the laughter and singing I always heard around your house."

"She was a prostitute, Helen. Your father didn't want his daughter involved with the bastard son of a prostitute. You can't hold that against him."

"I can and I will. Who made him God? Your mother successfully rose above that and worked her hands off trying to stay above it. There's no shame in that. And according to Doreen's notes, he wasn't above trying to take advantage of your mother's previous occupation. I'm sure it was her refusal that drove him to take it out on you."

Helen turned and walked across the room. "I feel dirty and guilty just thinking about my father treating you, your mother, and your family so shabbily."

"There is no such thing as 'the sins of the father', Helen. I'm not responsible for the birthright I was born into and you are not responsible for your father's actions. All we can do is rise above them. That's all in the past. We have found each other after all these years. Please don't let the past ruin the future. I love you and I know you love me. Isn't that enough?"

She stayed where she was looking at him. Her eyes met his, and then roved over his mouth, his hair, and his outstretched arms. "Do you have any idea how much I love you, this moment? This very instant?"

"I do. I trust your love, Helen. Please trust mine. Let's throw Doreen's diary in the fireplace and never bring it up again."

"I just wish there was some way I could make it up to your mother and Doreen."

"You already did. Doreen saw us get married and I'm sure she's told my mother all about it."

She picked up Doreen's book and looked at the gas fireplace. "I want to bury it with my father next time we're in the Soo. That's where it belongs, buried with the dead. You're right. No one else need ever know what's inside those covers."

He held her eyes with his. Dark brown eyes mirrored by dark brown eyes.

"Let's go for a walk along the canal then have a nice dinner out."

"Sounds perfect. Then we're coming home and I'm taking you to bed where I'm going to make love to you, then again, and again and again."

# Chapter Thirty-three

"Helen, you look a little under the weather this morning." Sarah trumped Margaret's ace of spades.

"On the contrary, I think she looks like a satisfied woman. Aside from a little darkness under the eyes, she looks fantastic." Olivia managed to win the next trick.

"Helen? You're not saying anything."

"Yes, she is. She's smiling." Olivia always seemed to pick up on Helen's moods.

"Let's just say I am blest with the best husband in the world."

"You two are still behaving like a couple of newlyweds. It's shameful." Margaret winked at Helen.

"So how are Gerald's niece and her husband doing with the baby?"

"They're in heaven. Stella sure brought a happy resolution to that dilemma."

Olivia dealt the cards. "I guess even Nicholas couldn't argue with that arrangement. Have you heard from him lately?"

"Yes, he doesn't say much about the situation, other than he has no reason to go to Sault Ste. Marie so it really doesn't affect him. He just needs time. They want Gerald and me to fly out for a week or two while Benjamin is still on summer break."

"Good thing you've got good luggage because it's certainly getting a workout. Good thing you sold your business because you would have had no time for it."

"How is that working out with you and Stella, Olivia?"

"I have to give that woman credit. She sure has a business head on her shoulders. I'm there for another month or two but she doesn't really need me."

"Maybe she'll let you go early. If she doesn't need you she may be happy to lose that payroll expense."

"The thing is, I'm enjoying it. Enjoying her. I feel badly that we made fun of her. She's quite a nice woman. She doesn't talk about it but I don't think she's had an easy life. She's good with people and very sympathetic to their needs. Like you, Helen, she goes out of her way to find them the right job."

"I'm glad to hear that, Olivia. She's certainly been kind to me even though I stole Gerald from her. Although, I must say we haven't received any baking lately."

"She's too busy to bake. I think the whole cooking thing just filled a void in her life that's now been filled with her productive business. I don't think she was really looking for men."

"So Helen's got a hunk of a husband who's keeping her happy. Olivia is happy with her new job. That leaves you and me, Margaret. What say we join a fall bowling league and see if we can find ourselves a hunk?"

Margaret didn't respond.

"Margaret?"

All eyes turned to her and cards were set down. "Okay, give it up. What's going on? You've been holding out on us haven't you?"

Margaret blushed. "I guess you've all been too busy to notice that I haven't complained of any stomach ailments lately."

# Acknowledgements

Many thanks to all my friends and acquaintances, old and new, who provided me with inspiration and fodder for this story; my talented book designer, friend and critic, Sherrill Wark at Crowe Creations; the Centrepointe Writing Circle in Ottawa who kept me on track with honest critiques and suggestions; and to my family who show me understanding and encouragement when I escape inside my cocoon to write.

# About the Author

Phyllis Bohonis grew up in Thunder Bay, where she met and married her first love. Still happy after all these years, they now live in rural Ottawa. Phyllis takes her writing from places she's been and people she's met, or not met, in her travels across Canada and the United States.

Her previous novels include *Fire in the Foothills*, *The Wilderness*, and *Tomorrow's Promise*. All are available in print or e-book through Amazon.com, Amazon.ca, or through your favourite on-line booksellers. You can order signed copies through her website www.phyllisbohonis.com. Phyllis's latest suspense/ thriller *The Track* will be available during the winter of 2016–17. Watch for the next book in the *73 Windsor* series in 2017.

A peek at the second book in the

# 73 Windsor Series

"So you've found a hunk?"

"And you haven't told us about him? What kind of friend are you?" Olivia tried to look upset but the gleam in her eye said differently.

Margaret looked around the bridge table. All eyes were on her. "Well, I wouldn't say he's a hunk, exactly."

"Yeh, yeh. He has a great personality and an even greater sense of humour." Sarah smiled as she folded her hand and moved it to one side. "Come on, give us the nitty gritty. All of it."

Helen placed her hand on Margaret's wrist. "Start at the beginning.

"I know you've all been bored to death with my seemingly never-ending list of ailments. You told me all I needed was a man in my life. "

"So you went out and got one? Way to go, Margaret!"

"Sarah, let her finish."

"Yes." Olivia agreed. "Let her finish. I want to hear the good part."

"All I'll say is you were right. Since I met Clarke I've not had a thing to complain about. I've never felt healthier."

She was positively beaming. The three women didn't take

their eyes from her. She didn't care. Let them wait. Whether she and Clarke were sleeping together was no one's business but their own. In the meantime she would have some fun with her friends. Not mischievous by nature, she felt they deserved a little teasing. It was Olivia that had told her the only thing that would get rid of her hypochondria was to get laid. After years of playing bridge every Thursday afternoon, they were more sisters than friends. She knew they'd had some good-natured fun at her expense. It was time to turn the tables.

"Clarke and I met about seven weeks ago. He was drawn to me immediately and instigated the conversation. I can't tell you how happy I am that he did. It didn't take long to realize we have a lot in common. He's not sexy looking. Definitely not a hunk. In fact he's rather … insignificant. Deceiving as that is, he's the best thing that's happened to me in a long time. Girls, I can guarantee you I won't be having any more stomach problems."

"Does Clarke, the superman, have a last name?" Olivia was standing, leaning against the kitchen doorway with her arms crossed in front of her.

"Ingram."

"Where does he work?"

"Retired."

Helen's eyes hadn't left Margaret's face.

"Do you have a question, Helen?"

"When are we going to meet Clarke Ingram?"

"Not for a while. He's visiting his grandchildren in southern Ontario for a few weeks."

"A few weeks? Are you going to survive without him for that long?"

"Don't worry, Sarah. He took very good care of me before he left." Margaret's wistful smile only added to their startled expressions. Finally she shook her head and stood. "It looks like we're not playing anymore bridge so I'll get that cheesecake and coffee out here."

"You can't just leave us hanging, Margaret. That's not fair. We need details."

"Sorry, girls. That's all you're getting."

CPSIA information can be obtained
at www.ICGtesting.com
Printed in the USA
LVHW04s1220230818
587579LV00005B/18/P